Suburban Souls

Maria Espinosa

TP

TAILWINDS PRESS

Excerpts from this work previously appeared in *The Magnolia Review*, Volume 5, Issue 2 (July 2019), and the *Adelaide Literary Magazine*, No. 31 (December 2019).

Tailwinds Press
P.O. Box 2283, Radio City Station
New York, NY 10101-2283
www.tailwindspress.com

Published in the United States of America
ISBN: 978-1-7328480-2-3
1st ed. 2020

for Judith Stephens

Suburban
Souls

PROLOGUE
Spring, 1961

Mirages rose on the endless concrete, shining glimmers that vanished as the car loomed closer. Air coming through the open window ruffled her hair, as golden as the fabled land of California. "My skin is so dry in this desert air," Gerda said. He patted her hand. "You're beautiful," Saul reassured her.

Huge clouds began to cover the desert sky. Raindrops splattered against the windshield. She thought of how they had first met on a rainy day in Chicago, in a crowded cafeteria. "May I sit down?" he asked. He gestured to the empty chair opposite her. "Yes," she said. Her beauty lured him, and for her part she was drawn to his air of quiet strength and the kindness in his dark eyes.

Rain came down harder. A strong wind rose. Rain blurred the desert landscape. Sparse bushes swayed in the wind. The car sped on towards the unknown where they would build their lives, far from grimy city streets and burdens of the past.

1.
April, 1975

The moon shone brightly through the curtains. Full moon. Gauzy curtains. Queen bed. Elsewhere in the house the children slept. He lay heavily over her body. He smelled of his own odor and of men's cologne. His face was focused with effort, his eyes closed as if he were imagining someone else as he rose above her like a warrior. Was he imagining his former sweetheart? The one who had jilted him? Or a forbidden blonde *fraulein* from his childhood? He thrust deep inside her, again and then again.

He gave a final thrust and then remained quiet, his sex still hard, and her body quickened into spasms, and something in her, too, released, and she gave a deep sigh. He wrapped his arm beneath her neck, pillowing her. "Did you come?" His voice held an unaccustomed tone of tenderness.

"Yes," she murmured.

He rolled over, his back curled against her, and soon he began to snore, while she lay awake and gazed at the beam of moonlight. Desire still ran through her body. A nameless fear seized hold of her.

Clinging to the comfort of Saul's warm body, she nudged him in the ribs.

"What is it?" he murmured.

"Tell me everything will be all right."

"Yes," he mumbled.

"Saul, tell me."

"How do I know? Gerda, let me sleep."

For a long time she lay awake. She bit her lips to keep from screaming. Finally she went into their bathroom and washed off the liquid between her thighs. Examined herself in the mirror. Haggard face. Dark eyes. Wild blonde hair. Took a sleeping pill from the cabinet and swallowed it. Wandered into the kitchen. Three A.M. The moon shone even more brightly in the kitchen, lighting up the stainless steel appliances, the stove, the refrigerator. Shining instruments. Pitiless, she thought. Pitiless and shining.

2.

The alarm rang at six A.M. Saul got out of the warm bed while his Gerda slept on, breathing softly. A strap of her nightgown had slipped. On impulse, he softly kissed her bare shoulder, but she didn't stir. He went into the bathroom, pissed, brushed his teeth, and splashed his face with cold water. Dressed quickly. Gulped down a glass of grapefruit juice. Grabbed his briefcase, and walked down the hill where he waited for the Van under a pale dawn sky.

While his seatmate leafed through pages of the *San Francisco Chronicle*, Saul turned to a novel by Amos Oz. It made him nostalgic to read about Jerusalem and life on a kibbutz, although such a different one from where he had spent the war years. After a while he dozed off, his finger still marking the page. While he slept, the Van rolled along the freeway, past stark clusters of beige stucco houses that rose above hills still green with spring growth.

Lulled by the motion of the vehicle, he dozed off again and slipped into a dream. When he woke up, it left a disturbing sensation. He couldn't remember the details, but it involved Gerda and the two girls when they were much younger.

Perhaps she wasn't meant to raise children. Perhaps it had been a mistake to leave Chicago and tear her away from all that was familiar. Esther, their younger daughter, had hardened herself. Early on, she decided that her father was her savior. She was a beautiful little girl with a serious expression and long dark curls. When she was four, she had snuggled up to him on the couch and confided, *I love you Daddy. Can I marry you when I grow up?* In later years, faced with Gerda's outbursts of jealousy, she remained unmoved. Hannah was different. She was thin and gangly, with bold eyes. Her heart was too open. How would she fare in the world? The Van lurched to a stop. He stumbled into the April sunshine and selected a bicycle from among others on the rack. The brisk morning air fully awakened him by the time he had pedaled to the chemistry buildings.

When he entered his Lab he heaved a sigh of relief. His refuge five days a week! Far away from cares of household, wife, and children. To think that the government paid him, and paid him well! He had struggled to reach this position. So many years of education he had missed on the primitive kibbutz after he fled Germany. When he arrived in Chicago at the age of twenty-three, he still lacked a high school degree. Fluent in both German and Hebrew, along with a smattering of Arabic, he worked hard to become fluent in English. While he attended night school, he also held a full-time job. Later there were scholarships as well, but he still had to work to make ends meet.

His Lab was a large windowless room with pale green walls, overhead fluorescent lights, and long metal tables loaded with equipment. The lack of windows didn't bother him. A sink and counter took up the length of one wall. An alcove provided space for his large office desk and chair, as well as a small refrigerator and a hot plate. On the far wall he had pasted lusty photos from the pages of *Playboy* and *Penthouse*. Big-bosomed women with generous derrières, they revealed intimate parts of their anatomies and flashed welcoming smiles. He had begun clipping these photos when he was in his early twenties, newly arrived in the United States. Longing for a girlfriend, he would imagine scenarios with one or another of these beauties while he masturbated. Gerda didn't know about the photos. He had managed to keep them hidden all the years of their marriage. Even now he occasionally jacked off in the men's room or at home in the privacy of the bathroom, so seldom was Gerda willing to have sex. Their marriage was not what he had dreamed of. But the children! Their photos stood on his desk: tiny Adam in Gerda's arms three weeks after his birth, Hannah and Esther in their school photos. It was for all of them that he worked. They were what gave his life meaning.

He made himself a cup of instant coffee. Put the paper bag containing his lunch in the refrigerator. He had prepared it the night before: a turkey sandwich, an apple, and a Mars Bar. He took out a doughnut from the top shelf. As he drank his coffee and munched on the powdery sweet, he planned the day's work. He would continue titrating samples of fluoride compounds with one hundred milliliters of tetrachloride to see if the same result could be obtained using mercury rather than gold as a catalyst. Commercially, mercury would be far less expensive.

All morning he inserted minute quantities of various fluoride compounds into flasks which held liquid solutions—gold, pale yellow, deep-hued turquoise. When he finally took a break, he realized it was noon. During the lunch hour he normally ate, shaved, and paid bills. Colleagues might linger over lunch or even work out at the gym, but he earned his keep, by God, he worked! He didn't horse around! No sirree!

All afternoon he worked, again with no breaks, as he wanted to finish this series of experiments today. At four o'clock the phone rang. There was a click at the other end. It rang two more times, and each time he let it ring. Gerda's nervous calls. Anxiety attacks. Best to ignore.

3.

Gerda's day had not begun well. When the alarm rang at six A.M., she pretended to be asleep as Saul dressed for work. Once she heard the front door slam shut and knew that he had left for the day, she went into Adam's room. So small, so frail in his crib. She picked him up and held him close. Soft downy black hair. Wet diaper. Changed him so that he was clean and dry. Put on his stretchy yellow pajamas. Took in the smell of talcum powder and baby skin. She could hear the girls' voices through the walls.

She was still groggy from the pill as she carried him into the kitchen. He felt heavy in her arms. The morning light that streamed in through the kitchen windows was too bright, and it hurt her eyes. She strapped him down in the high chair next to the girls who were eating breakfast. Cornflakes. Orange juice. A few cornflakes had spilled onto the table.

"Good morning, Mom"… "Morning."

"Good morning," she said.

She gave each girl a swift kiss.

She put a bib on Adam and took his bottle out of the refrigerator. He began to cry. Esther reached out and held his hand. Gerda put his bottle in a pot of water to warm and watched the flame beneath it flicker. Prepared instant coffee. Poured a drop from the rubber nipple onto her wrist. Warm enough. He stopped crying when she put the bottle between his lips, and he began to suckle hungrily.

She sipped her coffee. Nerves jangled. Her head throbbed. She looked more closely at the girls. Hannah, who was thirteen, wore a lavender T-shirt with a ripped neckline, hoop earrings, and too much lipstick. The T-shirt clung to her breasts. Esther, two years younger, was also wearing a carefully ripped T-shirt, a black one. Their hair, dark like Saul's, hung long and loose over their shoulders.

Although there were times she felt as if she would burst with love for them, this morning she saw something that their innocent features were hiding, and they seemed like demons in disguise. Witches with malevolence in their eyes.

"You look like sluts!"

"Mom!" cried Hannah.

"Those T-shirts make you look like whores . . . Your hair! Your makeup! Those cheap earrings!"

"This is how all the kids dress!"

"You're not going to school like that!"

"Mom, you don't understand!"

The tone in Hannah's voice, a slight whine, a slight air of condescension, angered Gerda.

"Go to your room and change. Now!"

"No!"

"Why are you being so mean?"

Gerda slapped Hannah's face.

Hannah screamed and raised her fists. "Bitch!"

"What was that?"

"Bitch!" screamed Hannah.

Gerda lunged towards Hannah and gripped her hard.

Punish the little whore! Kill both of them!

"Stop!" cried Esther.

Hannah broke free, which caused Gerda to lose her balance and stumble. Hannah ran out the front door, while Esther stood absolutely still, as if under a spell. Then she walked slowly to the hall, where she picked up Hannah's backpack from the floor as well as the red sneakers Hannah had left behind in her haste. She put on her own sneakers, hoisted her own pack around her shoulders, and left the house.

Adam was wailing. He had thrown his bottle onto the floor. Gerda picked up the bottle and stuck it back on his tray. Handed him a gleaming silvery spoon to play with. Cleaned up the remains of the girls' breakfast. Stuffed a load of laundry into the washer.

Saul's housekeeper. That is what she was. *This unbearable present. I love and hate them. His coldness. This man who shares my bed and whose seed is embodied in these children.*

The Maytag washer went around and around in the adjoining laundry room. She listened to it in a semi-trance. She could pack a small suitcase and escape to the Caribbean. Lie in the sun with a nice brown-skinned lover and sip margaritas.

If she had been stronger, stood up against Tante Ursula and Oncle Otto. *An actress you want to be! Not under this roof!*

A truck honked outside. Diaper service.

Fuck the delivery man!

In her worn red velveteen slippers she plodded into the laundry room for the bag of dirty diapers and carried them out the front door. The delivery man, dark-haired with sallow skin and a long narrow face, exchanged them for the pile of clean diapers neatly wrapped in butcher paper.

"Morning, ma'am."

"Morning," she said blearily.

Inside the house again, she opened a jar of baby cereal and spooned a little into his tiny mouth. When he'd had enough, she wiped off his face and hands. She could hurtle this bundle of flesh in her arms onto the floor, smash his fragile skull. As if sensing her thoughts, Adam began to scream.

She rocked him in her arms to soothe him, then set him down in his play pen in a corner of the living room. Children: whip them together into a smoothie she might serve Saul, like a witch from *Grimms' Fairy Tales*. Strange, shocking thoughts. She loved them, yes she did. She shouldn't have flared up like that.

The stainless steel kitchen. Top of the line appliances. The banality of her life, while Saul was at work doing what he loved, protected by a barbed wire fence, thick walls, layers of secretaries and administrators. Isolate a woman in a suburban house. Akin to foot binding.

The phone rang. It was her friend, Barbara. Thank God for her! "Good morning, love." Barbara's voice, deep-throated and warm and still sober at this hour, came through the wires. "How are you doing?"

"I'm okay."

How to explain the voice inside her? The voice that swept through her with strange, forbidden thoughts?

"Why don't you come on over later? Bring Adam."

The idea was tempting. Barbara, warm and bosomy and welcoming, in her Berkeley household with her hippie roommates, her young boyfriend, the wild garden with its purple morning glories and the bathtub covered with ivy in the midst of the grassy lawn, Barbara with her good lentil soup, her avocados, her stained bathrobe. But she needed to get away from all that was familiar and confining, even Barbara.

"Would it be okay if I leave Adam with you for a couple of hours? I need to take care of some things."

Barbara hesitated. "All right, love."

4.

Gerda's heels clattered against the pavement. North Beach in San Francisco. Bracing air and fog. She could see the Marina and the murky Bay far below. Glittering neon signs. Smells of Italian and Chinese cooking. Shops that sold curios and advertised tarot readings. A huge sign featured Carol Doda, the bare-breasted nightclub dancer. She felt wicked. Wicked and free. Alone and free. She passed City Lights Bookstore, where another time she would like to browse. Here in the city she could invent another life. Be another person. Escape out of her skin. She shivered in her thin dress and cardigan. She wanted to dance, to float in the cold air.

A café beckoned her with its white tablecloths and elegant interior. She walked inside and sat down at a table by the window, where a red rose stood in a slender vase. She ordered a glass of chablis. Contemplated the rose with its soft petals. Clouds outside darkened. She watched people walk by. Beatniks in black turtleneck sweaters. Girls in Indian scarves and long skirts amidst elderly Chinese in warm, practical clothing. A chill wind blew through the open door, and she shivered, closed her eyes, and suddenly her mood of exultation changed, and everything grew dark and fearful.

Through the plate glass window she watched a man in his sixties, with grey-white hair, pass by. He walked rapidly, although with a slight limp. He wore a silk paisley scarf knotted at the throat, a tweed jacket, flannel trousers. She thought that he looked uncannily like her father! An older version of the father who had gazed down at her for the last time in her tiny bed when she was only four. Her father! He had died, hadn't he? No one knew for sure. Perhaps by some miracle he managed to escape from Germany.

Something seized hold of her and hurled her out onto the street. *Follow him,* cried the voice. "Hey, Miss, your bill!" yelled the waiter, but she broke into a run so as not to lose sight of the stranger. Her purse with its long shoulder strap banged against her hip. After a block she caught up, breathless from running, and slowed to a walk. She followed him into a tobacco store. She knew it was him. He had survived the Gestapo. He had escaped Berlin. He had escaped Germany alive that terrible winter during the war so many years ago, when she saw him for the last time. It was him. She knew it. Felt it in her bones.

He ordered Dunhill cigarettes. His accent was European, and he had her father's voice. Gerda brushed up against him. "Excuse me," she stammered, "Are you from Berlin."

He shuddered. "No," he said.

"My father was from Berlin ... You look like him ... his photo ... I thought perhaps you were ... " A torrent of words choked in her throat. She blurted out, "Your wife. Your daughter. They stayed behind."

"You've mistaken me for someone else!" His voice was

cold. But his eyes were the same curious light blue as her father's eyes. That much of him she remembered clearly.

"Why are you hiding?"

"Miss, I'm not who you think."

"Is she bothering you?" asked the cashier, an elderly man with white hair and bushy dark eyebrows.

"No, it's all right," he said. Then he moved close to the counter, lowered his voice, and conferred with the cashier in a foreign language that sounded like German. They were talking about her, and they gave her swift glances as if she were crazy. They might call the police and have her arrested. Frightened, she fled from the store.

She wanted to die! Sink down on the sidewalk, sink beneath it and die. Pound on that man until he confessed the truth of who he was. Finally she staggered up from the cold pavement and limped to a bar where she ordered a whiskey to settle her nerves. Take deep breaths. Only a stranger. But it *was* him. He was in hiding. Chaotic thoughts. What was real? Why did she have such a strong sense that it was him? Or was she crazy? Crazy with longing for something that she didn't even know.

She looked at her wrist watch. Four o'clock. Time had gone by so fast. Where was a phone booth? There at the corner. She rushed to it, stuck a quarter into the slot. Barbara's line was busy. Then she dialed Saul's work number several times, but there was no response.

As she drove home, she felt panicky. The traffic moved so slowly. A jam on the Bay Bridge. When she finally reached Barbara's house in Berkeley, it was four-thirty. A thin man with a shaven head answered the door. Barbara had gone out. Adam was on the filthy green shag carpet, and he was chewing on a cigarette butt. Horrified, Gerda lifted him up into her arms. Of course he was wet. He was hungry. She found his bottle in the fridge. Warmed it under the hostile gaze of the thin man, whose name he said was Ken, and she gave it to Adam to suckle while she carried him along with all his paraphernalia into the car. Stuck him in the back seat, pacified now with his bottle.

My daughter! All these years I have missed you!

She was weeping as she drove. Such sadness. She could barely see. Horns honked. "Lady, you just ran a red light!"

Oh shit! She wept, scared and shaky, as she drove on through the Caldecott Tunnel and east along the freeway with its whizzing, speedy traffic. In a dazed state, she arrived home.

5.

Gerda sat on the edge of the bed in her nightgown. In her anxiety, she clutched the mattress. Lately these spells had been coming over her.

"Saul," she said in a soft voice. "Tell me things will be all right."

He seemed so far away, although he was only on the other side of the room. He was putting on his pajamas. Pale, determined being that he was.

"Saul," she repeated. "Tell me."

"How do I know?" He finished tying the cord around his waist.

"Tell me!" A wave of anguish swept through her.

She was starving, cold, and thirsty, and she screamed and screamed and sobbed. Finally, when she had grown faint from weakness and had fallen into a hopeless sleep, her pink blanket curled tightly against her, she heard voices and smelled a woman's fleshy odor, and felt warm thick arms around her. Someone murmured, Poor thing, poor little thing. A miracle, they said, that she survived when a bomb had demolished the rest of the building, and her mother's body lay crushed beneath rubble.

"Tell me, Saul."

Slowly he walked across the room and held her in his arms, her breasts soft against his bare chest. She looked up, but his face was as impassive as a Nazi's.

"Will everything be all right."

He stroked her cheek in a momentary surge of pity and tenderness.

"Do you want fairy tales?"

"Can't you feel for me, Saul?" Tears streamed down her cheeks. She had gained weight since Adam's birth six months ago, and her cheeks were bloated. "Gerda, I'm not a fortune teller." Her tears were painful for him to endure. His muscles tightened with the effort to repress his own emotion.

Memories of *Kristallnacht* swept through him. His father, stoop-shouldered, led away by two SS officers from their third-floor apartment in Frankfurt. They had nearly taken Saul as well, but decided he was too young. The fear in the pit of his stomach. Would he ever see his father again? What would happen to the rest of them? His mother, tight-lipped, ordered them all to pray, while from below in the street a mob shouted for Jews' blood.

"Gerda, I'm not a fortune teller."

"Do you love me?"

"I love you."

"Tell me like you mean it." She grabbed his shoulders and clutched at him as if she were drowning.

He held her more tightly, but she burst into sobs.

"Just tell me, Saul, tell me everything will be all right."

He glanced at the illuminated clock on his bedside table. It was eleven-thirty.

"Gerda, I need to get some sleep. I have to go to work in the morning."

She pulled away, enraged. "Fuck your work! You and your fucking self- importance! You and your fucking job!"

He turned his back to her and strode out into the hallway. She followed, striking him with her fists. He clenched his teeth, repressing an urge to knock her to the floor, strangle her to stop that horrible voice.

"You're pathetic!" she cried, rage flowing out of her. "I heard how that woman you were so in love with dumped you, just before we met."

Nina. Soft. Glistening. Nina, so tender. Nina, whom he would always love.

"You're scaring the hell out of the children!"

"Fuck the children!"

She gave a piercing shriek, and then to his horror she began to bang her head against the wall.

"Gerda, stop!"

"No!"

He grabbed her again, and for a moment she rested in his arms. But when she looked at his face, it was cold and set and withdrawn into a secret space inside himself. And her rage grew until she was on fire with it.

She wrenched away from him and resumed banging her head repeatedly against the wall, and as she did so, a painting of a ship in a stormy ocean rattled above her in its frame. It had been a wedding gift. They had spent a long time hanging it. She had changed her mind about where to place it. She had finally exhausted his patience. *An inch higher, Saul. No, half an inch lower.* Enough Gerda! He had hammered in the nail. *It's still a little crooked. Change it yourself, then,* he said. But she was lazy, and of course she hadn't.

The painting rattled crazily.

It fell, banging her head.

"Gerda, stop! I'm calling the police!"

"Do whatever the fuck you want!"

She picked up a lamp from a table in the hallway and hurled it to the floor. The bulb smashed into glistening fragments of glass that scattered onto the back of the painting.

"Mom, what's wrong?" Hannah cried.

"Watch out for the glass!" Saul cried as Hannah and Esther peeked out from their room.

"I'll kill you!" Blackness all around her. Anguish.

Gerda rushed into the kitchen and grabbed a knife from the cutlery rack. Hannah, who had followed her into the kitchen, stared at her with a pale face, as if frozen. Gerda lurched towards her, and Hannah rushed back into the bedroom.

Saul tore the knife away from Gerda and flung it across the room, then gripped her in his arms to restrain her as she struggled against him. Still holding her, he managed to dial 911 and contact an operator, while the girls lay on Esther's bed and held each other's hands. They scarcely dared to breathe. Esther said a prayer under her breath.

A few minutes later they heard the crunch of tires on the gravel driveway. Voices. Lights shone outside, followed by heavy knocks at the door. Three policemen stood there in all their heavy gear.

Saul released her from his grip in order to let them in the door.

She screamed and hurled herself towards the policemen, again brandishing the knife. One of the policemen knocked it out of her hand, and she fell. She kicked and screamed as they flipped her over onto her stomach, pulled her hands behind her back, handcuffed her wrists, and hoisted her up to a standing position.

"You fucking bastards!"

"Fucking idiot bastards!"

"DAMN YOU BASTARD SADISTS!"

They dragged her out the door, half carrying her as she went limp in their arms. Her screams began again, louder and piteous as they pushed her into the back seat of the police car.

One of the officers talked for a moment with Saul. Then they drove rapidly off.

The girls crouched in the doorway of their room, hidden in the shadows.

Afterwards, bursting with sadness, Saul went into their bedroom. He sat on the edge of Hannah's bed, and he put his arms around each of them. "It will be all right," he said, speaking words of comfort he had not been able to give his wife.

"Where did they take her?"

"To a hospital."

"Will she get better?"

"Yes," he said.

But Esther was silent, her face pursed in thought.

"I don't know if she will," she murmured, echoing his own fears. "It will be all right," Saul said again. "I'll take care of you." Somehow he could express a depth of tenderness for his children that he was unable to summon for his wife. He kissed them each good night, then went into Adam's room to check on him. The baby whimpered and stirred restlessly. Saul rocked him in his arms until Adam's head drooped in sleep.

6.

The gentle wife of whom he once dreamed. The memory of Nina. A wound that never healed. Nina of the dark eyes, the glistening skin, the pear-shaped breasts, the smile that won his heart. Her quality of listening. With three children . . . no, never would she have acted like this.

Although he was enraged with Gerda, at the same time he pitied her as he lay awake and the hours passed. No sleep. No work tomorrow. Who would care for Adam? The girls? How long would she be in the psych ward? Would she ever be okay? Would he be saddled with this crazy harridan for the rest of his life?

"She is not the right one," his mother had said. "I want so much that you marry and raise a family—high time now that you have a good job—but she is not the one. Something is not right with her." She stood in the sunny dining room of their Chicago apartment with its mahogany furnishings. His mother: stolid and lumpy-bodied, in the auburn wig that she wore as an Orthodox woman. His mother who had somehow rescued his father from the clutches of the SS and had managed to get them all out of Germany.

A strain of music hit his ears from the classical station

on the radio. Mozart piano concerto. So beautiful and sad, almost unbearably so, while at the same time crystalline. He would like to have known Mozart. Perhaps they would have been companions. In another life he, Saul, might have been a composer, a pianist.

The romantic core beneath his tough sabra hide.

He had to be tough. Men don't cry. Images rose up of the nighttime landing of their refugee ship, at a hidden harbor outside of Haifa. A faint moon. Brilliant stars. Lonely years on the kibbutz, while he worried if his family, far off in Chicago, were still alive. Early morning light shone into the bedroom. Perhaps he had dozed. Alarm rang. Get up. Wash face. Coffee. Girls somber in the kitchen. Adam in his high chair was making a mess with his bowl of oatmeal.

"My fault," sobbed Hannah. "I was so mean to her."

"Not your fault," said Saul. "Don't cry."

Esther patted her sister's hand. "It's not our fault. She's crazy."

"She is *meshugah,*" said Saul in an upsurge of rage. He wiped oatmeal off Adam's face with a napkin. Adam waved his spoon in the air. "Da ... Da," he smiled endearingly.

7.

Gerda woke up in a narrow bed with metal sidebars and stiff white sheets. The hospital gown she was wearing itched. Where were her clothes? Her head hurt, and she felt groggy. She had a vague memory of the night before. Perhaps they had drugged her. The room, barely more than a cubicle, had pale green walls, and there was a smell of Lysol. Bright lights shone overhead. A middle-aged woman sat on the edge of the bed across the room, a fat blonde in a flowered housecoat. She stared at Gerda with hostile eyes.

Trying to ignore the other woman's presence, Gerda slowly pulled herself out of bed, hoisted herself over the protective bars, stood up, and walked unsteadily across the creaky linoleum floor to the open doorway. An aide in a pale blue tunic and white pants stood there.

"How are you?" asked the aide.

"I feel like shit," said Gerda. "Why am I here?"

"The doctor will talk to you about that," said the aide in a crisp voice.

"When will I see him?"

"Later today."

"I want to go home."

She felt frantic, panicky, helpless.

Two more aides now appeared on the scene, all three arrayed against her.

"I want to go home," she repeated.

"Come and have some breakfast, dear," said the oldest one, a stocky woman with short grey hair.

"Fuck you!"

Ignoring her words, the grey-haired aide took Gerda's arm and forcefully guided her to the dining area, which had a cafeteria-style counter and a room with small round Formica-topped tables. About twenty men and women were there, some in pastel hospital gowns—Gerda looked down at her own horrible pink gown—and others in sweatpants or jeans or bathrobes. They sat at the tables, eating, chatting, or gazing into space like zombies.

In a furious haze, Gerda sipped coffee and pecked at a bowl of dry corn flakes.

Later she wandered into the day room of her ward, where women and girls with glazed looks sat on worn couches and chairs, transfixed by flashing images on the large-screen television. Why was she locked up here? Blurred memories of the previous night swirled through her brain. Police. Handcuffs. Distraught girls. And Saul, hard-faced. She stared out of the window at a large bush with spiky leaves, then looked around the room for some diversion.

There was nothing to read except old issues of *Woman's Day, House Beautiful,* and *Seventeen. Seventeen* for aging women? For one or two young girls in the ward, wounded birds?

An aide appeared with Gerda's red patent leather overnight suitcase, the one she had brought to the delivery room at Kaiser Hospital for each of her children's births. "Your husband brought you some clothes," she said. Gerda went back to her room and changed. Saul had brought her old blue woolen sweater, jeans, three T-shirts, underwear, socks, and sandals, along with toothbrush, hair brush, comb, and lipstick. The paperback novel by Marilyn French that she'd been reading (that was thoughtful of him—but how long did he think she was going to be here?). She flung her flimsy hospital gown onto the floor, lay down on the bed, and wept.

Later that day a psychiatrist with a round face, receding hair, and rimless glasses interviewed her. He had the air of a choir boy, she thought. A voyeur peering obscenely into a woman's private life.

"I don't belong here," she said.

"You tried to kill your children."

"That's a lie!"

"Not according to the police report."

"My husband lied. I love my children. They're my life."

He lowered his glasses and wrote rapidly on a notepad.

She looked around her. Several framed diplomas hung on the otherwise bare walls. Through the window she could see maple trees. Their green leaves fluttered in the May breeze.

"I hate the suburbs," she said. "I'm a city girl. Raised in Chicago."

He said nothing, just looked at her, pen poised in his hand.

"Well, damn, say something, doctor! You're like my husband. His silences drive me wild . . . I give and give and give . . . I'm bored to death, cooped up with children all day, so I drink a little, and he calls me an alcoholic."

"Are you?" He looked up from his notes.

"Well, what if I am? I drink too much. He drives me to it. Drives me to drink." She giggled in spite of herself. She glanced at the photo of his wife and children in a gilt frame on his mahogany desk, then asked, "Does your wife drink, too?"

"That's not relevant."

Little Suburban Wifey and her Brood. She had an urge to smash the photo, such a strong urge that she clenched her fingers.

"That photo . . . Your wife and children?" she asked in a weak voice.

"Yes," he said.

She burst into tears.

He sat quietly, pen in hand, then gave her a Kleenex. A gentler look came over his face.

She took the Kleenex, felt the warmth of his hand, and her sobs burst out afresh. "I want to go home," she sobbed. "When can I go home?"

"Gerda, you're on seventy-two hour hold."

"Why?"

"It's the law."

"It's not fair. It's just not fair!"

"It's the law," he repeated. Once again his face became impassive, a mask.

On his desk, next to the horrid Wifey and Brood, was a heavy green glass paperweight shaped like a frog. She picked it up and held it aloft.

"You'd better put that down."

She put it down hard on the desk, and her hand was shaking.

"It's too much," she sobbed. "It's all too much."

"What is too much, Gerda?" he asked gently.

"It's just all too much."

Three days passed. On a cold rainy afternoon at two P.M., Saul came for her. She was pale and trembling when he met her in the lobby, where an aide waited with her.

He kissed her softly on the lips, a dry gentle kiss.

"Feeling okay, honey?" he asked with unusual gentleness. At that moment his heart opened; he felt the poignancy of her fall from grace; he felt her hurt, her pain, and he wanted to shelter her.

"Your wife is very fragile," the doctor had said, staring intently at Saul. "Her early life in Germany left its mark."

"I know," said Saul. "As Jews, we both suffered."

Frankfurt 1938. He was nine years old. Wooden shutters in the front room closed against the outside world. He could not see very much. Only dim light shone through the cracks. He was wearing heavy leather shoes and long, thick socks, leather *hosen* that came down to his knees, a scratchy linen shirt, and a sweater, as well as a yarmulke that his mother had knit. Trying to hide his fear, he descended the stairs to the street.

No sooner had he stepped outside than they saw him!

Too late to hide. He began running as fast as he could.

"Hey, a Jewish kid! Let's beat the crap out of him!"

He tore off his yarmulke and stuffed it into his pocket. Kept on running. Faster! Faster!

"Come on, don't let him get away . . . *Juden . . . Juden. Schwein!*"

Their voices sounded loud in the frosty air. Their footsteps pounded on the cobblestones. They were fair-haired boys his own age who wore the brown shirts and brown berets of the Hitler Youth Group.

He was out of breath and had a stitch in his side, but he kept on running. The yarmulke slipped out of his pocket and fell into a puddle. He stooped to pick it up and held it, sopping wet, in his hand, as he turned onto a side street.

Don't fight back, his mother had warned. Don't ever fight the *goyim* back. Yet she insisted that he wear the yarmulke in public. Each morning she planted it firmly on his head and gave his cheek a dry kiss. At his school with its earnest future Talmudic scholars, wearing it on the street was a badge of honor.

Their voices sounded closer. Their footsteps sounded louder against the cobblestones. He turned another corner into a narrow alley where rusty garbage cans stood in a row. He crouched behind the cans and scarcely dared to breathe, until at last their footsteps faded.

Don't look back. Be strong. Be like the sabra plant. Don't let your heart and your feelings show your vulnerability. He had learned that in Israel, where at last he was able to fight back!

That night he lay beside Gerda in bed and caressed her. He wanted to give her the tenderness she needed, wanted to feel it in his heart. She clung to him, dank with sweat, her perfume oppressive, but he did not dare remove her body from his. My wife, he told himself, mine to honor and cherish according to the Talmud. One of the six hundred and eleven rules for observant males. Love and honor thy wife. If only he could open his heart, his mind, and forgive her for the past, but he couldn't. He was hurt, paralyzed, filled with anger.

There was a time he had loved her. But all that was

long ago. He remembered a Sunday morning when Hannah was still an infant. Gerda had been squeezing fresh orange juice. He put his arms around her waist, feeling her rump, her warmth. She was wearing a low-backed yellow sundress. Her hair gleamed in the sunlight, and he had felt an instant of pure love for this woman who was sharing his bed, his life, and who had given birth to their child.

He remembered the radiance of her expression when she held Hannah, when she nursed her, breasts swollen with milk. She had been a different person then. They had been happy. They had been building a life together, a life that seemed full of promise.

During the following weeks, he tried to make it up to her. He took her to a concert with the San Francisco Symphony Orchestra, and they played selections from Mozart and Brahms, his favorites, and the beauty of the music swept through him. He grasped her hand. Her bright red nail polish gleamed in the soft light. She turned to him, a questioning look in her eyes. The music did not have the magic for her that it held for him, but she was glad that they were doing something together, something apart from the children, that he had cared enough to plan this evening's event.

8.

Thank God for Carmela, the cleaning woman who had cared for Adam during Gerda's stay at the hospital.

The girls were on their best behavior. They, too, liked Carmela. *If only she, Gerda, could be like this woman.* At times Gerda crushed the girls in her arms, murmured words of love, stroked their soft hair, and was overcome with tenderness. Their unnatural quietness and their whispers pained her. She hated their fear of her.

On weekday mornings the girls went off to school, backpacks slung over their shoulders. Saul was safely ensconced in his laboratory, far from the cares of the world. A good man, people said. She, Gerda, was bad. A bad woman. A bad mother.

Bad girl, Gerda. Bad seed. Like your father. The swift blow across the face. The woman, whom she called Tante Ursula, dragged her into the closet and turned the key. It was dark and cold. She clutched her arms for warmth. These people were not her real parents. They had rescued her from the Red Cross orphanage and taken her to America. Perhaps it would have been better if they had never found her.

"You're not a bad seed," said Barbara, who sat across

from her at the round table crowded with food and unwashed dishes. They were sitting in the kitchen of Barbara's old two-story house in the heart of downtown Berkeley. It was two-thirty on a weekday afternoon, and Adam lay strapped in his baby carrier on the kitchen counter, blessedly asleep while the women talked.

From the basement came pulsing sounds of Barbara's teenage son's band, which was rehearsing rock music. Adam stirred, but did not awaken.

Barbara, large and bosomy, with long black hair, luxuriant features, olive skin, and a warm, sultry voice, sipped her wine. Gerda took a sip of hers. Cheap Gallo mixed with the aroma of a beef casserole that simmered on the stove.

A young man in his twenties, with a lock of blond hair that fell across his forehead, walked into the kitchen, bent down and kissed Barbara's neck. "Honey," she said, "You know Gerda."

"Oh yeah, we've met."

He caressed her shoulder. She held his fingers, then let go. He went to the stove, helped himself to a bowl of casserole, and left.

"You're not a bad seed," Barbara repeated. She took another sip of her wine. "It's your husband who's a jerk."

"No, he's not. Underneath he's good," said Gerda, suddenly defensive.

"He would drive me bananas."

Barbara gazed past Gerda at the large black and white photograph of herself that hung on the wall, a young and glamorous version of herself in the fifties. At the time she had been acting in an off-Broadway play. Now she directed local theatrical productions.

"Gerda, I wish you'd try out for the Strindberg play. You'd love it."

"I can't."

"You used to act. I know you love the stage!"

"I only acted in one play in college. A small part." She laughed in embarrassment. "Then there's Adam. I need to be home with him."

"Let Saul take over at night."

"No, he wouldn't like that."

"Are you going to let yourself keep on being a slave to that man?"

"You're right! But Saul . . . Saul . . . " She fumbled for words. Against his strength, his stubbornness, the financial power that he wielded, she felt powerless.

Barbara leaned forward and suddenly asked in a conspiratorial voice, "Did you plan Adam?"

"That's a cruel question!"

"He's so much younger than the girls."

"I don't want to talk about it." She rose from her chair.

"Don't go off mad, Gerda."

"I've gotta get home."

"Think about trying out for a part."

"I can't."

"You mean your husband won't let you! He is a jerk. He was so cold when I met him. I don't think he respects you."

"But he does!" cried Gerda.

"You're confused, honey."

"Yes, I am confused."

Gerda downed the rest of the wine in her glass. She wanted to get out of here! Adam gave a soft cry, as if echoing her thoughts. She took her sweater from the back of the chair, put it around her shoulders, and lifted up Adam in his carrier. "Gotta go."

"A slave to that man!"

"Yes!" shouted Gerda, enraged. Her friend was betraying her! Only Saul was steadfast, no matter his coldness.

9.

At times Hannah hated her mother. "She's outrageous," said her sister, Esther. "I just make my face cold when she tries to kiss me. I hate her all the time."

"Sometimes I love her," said Hannah. "Sometimes she's nice. She can understand me better than anyone else. I think that's her real self underneath."

"Oh?" In Esther's mind, her older sister, Hannah, was her real mother, the one she turned to for comfort. Hannah was the one who loved her and shielded her.

But Hannah loved Gerda, and it cut her to the heart when Gerda was going through one of her crazy, mean spells. Hannah instinctively fought back, trying somehow to bring her mom to her senses.

On Hannah's thirteenth birthday, Gerda spent the day alone with her. They went across the Golden Gate Bridge for a long drive through Marin County, and Gerda chatted happily as they drove. She seemed like a young girl again. They stopped at a bluff above Muir Beach, where a cold ocean breeze swept through them, and then they drove back to the upscale rustic restaurant they had passed earlier.

"We look like sisters," Gerda said with a smile when they stood in front of a mirror at the entrance of the restaurant. In truth, the two of them did resemble each other in their posture and features, although Gerda was blonde while Hannah had inherited her father's dark hair. They both wore jeans, sweaters, and Birkenstock sandals. Hannah was smaller-boned than her mother, a gangly teenager. Her eyes shone with the light of youth, while Gerda's face had begun to show lines of age. But today her eyes, too, shone with happiness.

For lunch they ordered rare hamburgers with pickles and all the trimmings, and milkshakes—vanilla for Gerda, chocolate for Hannah—relishing their time together in the crowded, sunny dining room.

"You're my favorite child," Gerda said as they ate. "You're the only one who truly sympathizes with me."

"I know, Mom," said Hannah. Her mom's words made her uneasy. "What about Esther?"

"She's stronger than you. Her heart is cold."

"No it isn't!" cried Hannah, loyal to her sister. "She's just more scared of you. And sometimes you scare me."

"I don't want to scare you, my darling," said Gerda, her eyes brimming with love and sadness. "I love you so much."

"Then don't hurt me."

"Sometimes I just get overwhelmed. Something takes over . . . I don't know what . . . Something just rips through me."

"You have it easy, Mom. You're not working at a job. Carmela comes in to help. You've got Dad, and you've got us. Don't you love us at all, Mom?"

"Of course I do. But sometimes . . . I have memories. My father left when I was so young, and they say he died in a camp. I used to imagine what it would be like if he and my mother had raised me. My aunt and uncle never understood children or American ways.”

“It must have been hard for you,” said Hannah. She herself was a little frightened of Tante Ursula.

Gerda gazed past Hannah. “Before your father, there was someone else,” she said, deliberating her words. “Perhaps I would have been happier with him.”

“But what about *us?* We wouldn’t have been born,” said Hannah. She felt sick in the pit of her stomach. She looked into her mother’s eyes. “Why didn’t you marry him?”‘

“Many reasons. This is a secret between the two of us, Hannah. Your father doesn’t know.”

“I don’t like secrets!”

“Damn you!” Gerda exploded. “I trust you, and you throw it in my face.”

Hannah burst into tears, rushed into the bathroom, and wept.

Later Gerda tried to make it up to her daughter. “This is your special day! Your birthday! The day you came into the world I was so happy. You were the daughter I wanted.”

They parked on the slope of Mount Tamalpais. As they hiked along a trail that led up the mountain, the tall, beautiful redwoods, the greenery, the scent of pine needles and wild flowers and laurel, along with the clean mountain air, all helped Hannah shake off the feeling that her mother’s confession had aroused in her.

10.

For a time their household was peaceful. Adam was beginning to crawl on all fours, and to speak a few words. The girls loved to play with him. With them, his smile would brighten, and he would laugh at their games. This took some of the burden off Gerda.

Saul would hold him in his lap in the evening, and he displayed a charming boyishness that he had only with very young children. Sadly, to Gerda's mind, only when the children were young was Saul that uninhibited. He would toss Adam gently up into the air and sing German folk songs to him. He displayed a tenderness with the baby and the girls that warmed her heart and also tormented her because he was often so brusque with her.

One night during Memorial Weekend in late May, the family gathered outside in the garden to wait for the fireworks. It felt peaceful. If only it could always be this way, thought Saul. Adam nestled in Gerda's arms while she lay back on a blanket, and the girls, the lights of Saul's life, nestled close to their mother as if protecting her. He sat with his knees hunched against his chest, a little apart from them so that he could smoke his pipe without the smoke blowing in their faces. The grass was damp with dew, and the windbreaker beneath him provided protection. The evening air was fresh. A breeze ruffled the leaves of the maple tree by the fence. Then the fireworks began, and sparkling showers of fiery color rose in the distance over the Oakland hills.

Adam felt too heavy in Gerda's arms. She shifted his weight and put him down on the blanket beside her. She gazed up at the few stars that shone, dimmed by lights of the suburbs. As she gazed at them, her thoughts were far away.

11.

Gerda stumbled over a crack in the sidewalk. A firm hand steadied her. "Thank you," she said. She turned to her rescuer. A dark-haired man in turtleneck and jeans, a diamond in one ear, striking features. A poet perhaps or a beatnik—now the term would be hippie. One of the many who lived here in San Francisco's North Beach. "No problem," he said. "Hey, you're a pretty lady." She flushed, "I'm married." She turned, hastened her gait to get away from him, and fled into the City Lights Bookstore. She had lost him. Good! But what if she had smiled and looked into his eyes? What if she had not brushed him off? No—he wasn't that attractive with his acne-pitted complexion, and he smelled unwashed. Still, he had looked interesting. In a semi-daze she wandered through narrow corridors of books into an alcove and found herself gazing at German literature. Titles in the original language and in translation: Gunther Grass. Rilke. Heinrich Heine. Hesse. The language of her earliest memories.

If only she could take refuge here, venture out for a little food, and sleep here, hidden, at night. Musty smell of books. A young woman, thin, dark hair pulled back, glasses, stood looking at German periodicals in the corner.

Then she saw him. He wore a light-weight tan leather jacket, the same paisley scarf knotted at the throat, and had a bald spot on the back of his head that she had not noticed before. Pinkish skin. Stubble on his face, as if he had neglected to shave for a few days. Something downcast about him, as if he had been going through a rough spell. The same package of Dunhill cigarettes protruded from his rear pocket that she had seen him purchase weeks ago.

"*Sprecken zie deutsch?*"

He turned around and flushed when he saw her. "You again!"

"So you are German!"

"What of it!"

"You humiliated me the last time we met. Are you afraid I will expose you?"

He flushed. "So, little stalker, you followed me."

"No, I didn't."

She came closer. She was wearing a low-cut summery dress. A bouffant muslin, white with a print of green sprigs. She had combed her unruly hair so that it hung loose, a blonde cloud around her face. And before leaving the house, she had dabbed on a bit of Chanel No. 5.

"You followed me."

"No," she repeated.

"So then why are you so conveniently here?"

"I just came to look at books."

She reached out and boldly grasped his hand. "I know you are him." She was under a spell, in a trance as though she had entered another reality, as if she were in a dream from which she did not want to awaken.

He surveyed her with a changed expression. She became aware that he was scrutinizing the cleavage between her breasts on the low-cut neckline, surveying her hips, her thighs that were outlined beneath the thin material of her dress.

She kept hold of his hand. Noted the fingers, shaped like her own but longer. His skin was soft, the back of his hand liver-spotted.

"Do you remember the four-year-old you left behind?"

"Did you hire a detective, little stalker?"

He drew her close and gave her a swift, passionate kiss on the lips. "Incest," he murmured.

She drew back. "No!"

"Then why do you come dressed for sex if you're looking for a daddy?"

His accent was thicker than Saul's slight accent, which people barely noticed.

"You abandoned us!"

He looked straight into her eyes.

"Lower your voice! Act like you're not crazy. Since you won't leave me alone, let's get out of here before they throw you out." He gripped her wrist and led her to the front counter where he paid for a volume on German postwar history, a thin paperback bound with a white cover, and he stuck it into the inner pocket of his jacket.

"Come with me," he said.

Mute like a lamb, she followed this man who was only pretending not to be who he was. The day had grown chilly. She shivered. Wind had risen. It blew her skirt and ruffled her hair. She followed him into an alley and into a small hotel with a sign in French above the door, *"La Petite Auberge."* Through the hallway with faded yellow walls that smelled of cooking odors and mustiness. Up two flights of winding creaky stairs. Inside his room.

Double bed with wrought-iron frame. Heavy damask purple drapes partially covered a window through which she could see the back of another building and a patch of grey sky. A desk littered with papers and an ashtray overflowing with cigarette butts. Strong odor of tobacco. A cluttered bureau. Photos. She looked at them. Unfamiliar faces. A woman with dark hair and two babies in her arms.

"What have you done with memories of my mother?"

Still inside the dream.

"A pigpen, this room!"

"So, little stalker, a father complex!"

"Don't bullshit me."

He embraced her, kissed her roughly on the lips, thrust his hand inside her dress. She pulled away. "Fuck you! Get away from me!"

"Why did you come with me, little stalker, if not to get laid?"

"You are my father! You're just lying. Pretending. I could expose you and get you arrested for abandonment!"

He laughed. "Crazy lady!"

"I'm not crazy! You're the big liar! The big pretender! Covering up. I know you had to do that back in the war to survive. You ruined our lives!"

He grabbed her again, fondled her breast. Again she pulled away and grabbed scissors that lay on the desk.

"Don't come close to me. Stay away!"

"So you like it rough, *meine liebe,* little sweetheart."

He struck the scissors from her hand, pulled her close, and flung her down on the bed with its dark quilted spread. He smelled of tobacco and aftershave and sweat. He thrust his leg between her thighs. She shrieked, pushed with all her strength to get his heavy weight off her, and rushed to the door.

"Wait!" he cried. "Don't leave! I won't hurt you! Please please, stay! I won't touch you! I will respect your wishes!" She looked back. His eyes were wide, supplicating, and as he stared at her he reminded her of a forlorn dog. Lonely old man. As if echoing her thoughts, he said, "I am alone here. So alone. I used to be a musician in Munich. I still play sometimes. Not like the old days. Let me sing you a song."

He reached for a large red and white accordion perched on the floor beside his bed. He sat back against the pillows and began to play and to sing a familiar song, a German song that she remembered from childhood. He sang in a hoarse voice. She let go of the doorknob and stood there and listened. And then she joined him in the chorus. The two of them sang together. Something surged in her heart. She suddenly wanted to cry. She crept back onto the edge of the bed and continued to sing along with him. Her hip was touching his. And they sang on.

Komm lieber Mai, und mache
Die Baume wieder grun
Und lass uns an dem Bache

In May the trees grow green again, and the little
  violets bloom . . .

He paused. "You're a lovely woman," he said. "A bit crazy." He put down the accordion and caressed her hand, looked at the wedding ring. "If your husband loved you the way you need to be loved, you wouldn't be here."

She pulled her hand away. "Why not?"

"Do I need to explain?" He gave her a significant look, straight into her eyes, and gently stroked her hair. "You have a delicate spirit," he said. "Underneath that tough come-on."

No one had ever said that to her before. She wasn't really tough. The words that came out of her, even the blows that she struck against her children, all that was not her at all but something alien that tore through her.

He told her about his childhood on the outskirts of Munich, about how he fled Germany with a passport for England when he was seventeen. A scholarship to the University of London secured his passage. No, he was not her father! But perhaps he was a distant cousin. Surely with their features so similar, they must be related by blood. She felt an emotional warmth from him that she had never experienced before.

When she stood up at last to leave, he stood up too, and put his arms around her. She felt such a warmth emanating from his eyes, his body, his entire being. "Could you love me?" he asked.

She shook her head and pulled away.

All the way home she trembled as she sat by a window on the newly built BART. Yes, she wanted him. Her body was on fire with wanting him. Her head throbbed, and she had an urge to masturbate right there on the BART as the train rolled through the dark tunnel beneath the Bay. In her seat, alone, she clenched tight between her thighs, trembling with desire.

When she got home, she found Adam crawling around on the living room carpet, and dangerously close to the electrical outlets. She grabbed him just as he was about to stick his finger into an outlet. He cried out in protest. "Girls! Where are you? Why aren't you taking care of Adam? He nearly got electrocuted!"

Esther emerged from the hall bathroom. "I was just peeing."

"Where is Hannah?"

"I don't know. She went out."

"You should never leave him alone like this!"

"I'm sorry, Mom."

"Sorry won't do it!" She slapped Esther hard across her face. Esther burst into tears. Then Gerda grabbed Adam, still on the carpet. He was crying now with all the power in his lungs. She slapped him across the rear. "Take him!" she ordered. "Change him. And feed him."

In the kitchen she gulped down the contents of a partially full bottle of Jamesons. So close she had come! Now there was a real man who knew how to deal with her!

Her father . . . Maybe it really was him! Still in hiding after all these years. Inventing elaborate stories about his life. The room spun around her. Everything was crazy. She was leading a fake life. This was not her true life. Suppose she had lain with him, allowed him to ravish her, and had never returned to this dreary suburban outpost at the end of the world, with the false beacon of a friend like Barbara, an imposter, beckoning her?

12.

Thoughts about work filled Saul's mind as he walked home from the bus stop and up the narrow lane towards his house. As he came closer, he heard loud rhythmic music. The kind that his children loved and that left him cold. A blaring saxophone. A strident singing voice with choral backup.

I heard it on the grapevine . . .

about to lose my mind . . .

Gerda, dressed in a flimsy shift, was dancing unsteadily on the deck with Adam in her arms. "Hey, sweetie," she yelled, "Ready for a hot fuck?"

Heard it on the grapevine.

She stumbled. He rushed over and grabbed Adam from her arms. His briefcase, which he dropped in his haste, fell open, and papers scattered over the deck.

"Gerda!"

"Want a hot fuck, sweetie?" Her voice slurred the words slightly, and her breath smelled of alcohol.

"You've been drinking!"

"Well, just a little. What of it?" She giggled.

"You are not fit to be a mother! You nearly dropped Adam!"

"No? I'm not. Well, I can warm your brats in the oven if you like!" She loomed close, her face up against his, squashing the baby's body. Saul pulled away, and the baby squirmed in his arms.

Hannah and Esther watched from the doorway.

"Mom's bored," Hannah ventured in a small voice. "She says you're with stimulating people, while she's home all day."

Gerda rushed over to Hannah. "This one loves me!" she shouted triumphantly.

"Yes, I do, Mom," whispered Hannah, feeling her mother's anguish. "But I wish you wouldn't drink."

I drink to escape. The stranger's arms and body. I wish I had let him have his way with me.

"Mom is crazy," Esther muttered. "She's crazy." She went over to her father and gripped his arm, while he kept a firm hold of Adam.

Yeah! I heard it through the grapevine
Oh, I'm just about to lose my mind.

Family dynamics, thought Gerda in a flash of sobriety. "The two of you always gang up on me."

Saul, his lips compressed in rage, went inside the house, holding tightly to Adam who was sobbing in earnest by now, followed by Esther. "I'll take him, Dad," she offered.

Little goody two shoes. Gerda lurched forward, stumbled over an uneven plank, fell onto a mass of papers, and screamed out in pain as her ankle folded beneath her.

She limped into the house, went to the refrigerator, and got out ice cubes for her ankle. Saul turned off the music. While she lay on the living room couch with the bag of ice wrapped around her ankle, a magazine half open beside her, Saul fried eggs for dinner. Hannah picked up the papers on the deck and set the table in the kitchen. Esther played with Adam in the living room, then set him in his high chair, warmed up a bottle of milk, and fed him baby-bottled squash. The girls ate quietly, dominated by Saul's silent rage.

Afterwards Saul lay on the conjugal bed and kicked his heels in frustration. He wanted to yell at the top of his lungs. He wanted to beat the shit out of her! But he needed to get some sleep so that he would be fit to work in the morning. He tried to calm himself by visualizing numbers in his mind.

Her voice disturbed his meditation. "We need to talk," she said.

He turned on his side. She was lying next to him, and he could feel the silk of her nightgown as her body touched his, smell her familiar odor.

"You've talked enough, Gerda!"

"You dump all your anxiety on me."

"That's bullshit!"

"I pick up your anxiety, Saul. You dump it on me, and then you go merrily off to work while I'm left here at home, filled with it. At night you go to sleep, and I lie awake, filled with your shit."

"You're crazy."

"Saul, listen to me!" He rolled over on his stomach and put his hands over his ears.

"Say something, damn it!"

"Stop bugging me."

"You never listen to me."

"You talk too much," he said. Abruptly he sat up, smoothing the bedspread beneath him.

"Oh yes? Listen to me. You're a poor excuse for a man. Bottled up. Afraid to show emotion. And you dump on me with your pathetic cock! It doesn't satisfy me. It's too small. You don't know how to make love. You're not human, and you drive me crazy. If I'm a bad mother, it's your fault, and I'll kill your brats!"

Unable to stand it any longer, he got up from the bed. The luminous clock showed it was nearly midnight. Ignoring her furious stream of words, he put on a pair of trousers, a shirt, his shoes, and walked out of the house. Her cries followed him out onto the road. He walked, not knowing or caring where he was going.

"Hey, man," said a familiar voice. Stan, his next door neighbor. "Hey, man, you need to chill . . . Come on in . . . You need to chill," said Stan. "We hear her yelling every night . . . Every night we hear her . . . Come on in and mellow out."

In a daze, he followed Stan into his house. The living room had a stained rug, red floor cushions, dim lights. Music that Saul did not recognize. It was something with drums, a strong rhythm, a voice that sounded South American. There was a strong smell of marijuana. Stan's wife, Jill, a skinny blonde, clad only in white panties and a white T-shirt that showed her nipples, lay back against a faded beige couch. Her eyes were closed as she listened to the music. Stan lit a joint and held in the smoke for a moment, exhaled, and handed the joint to Saul, who followed his neighbor's example. He had never smoked marijuana before, and he was uncomfortable with Jill's state of undress, but he felt himself relaxing with the music and fell asleep. Later he rose with a start. Stan and Jill had passed out. It was still dark when he left their house, surprisingly hungry, and he crept into bed beside Gerda's sleeping body.

13.

"We need you, man," said Frank, his supervisor. "But your work has fallen off. What's going on?" Frank's kind eyes showed concern. His long legs dangled over the box of packing materials in Saul's Lab.

"I've been having a hard time at home."

"The secretaries gossip. I've heard about all those phone calls from Gerda. I imagine it's hard on you." Frank placed his warm hand briefly on Saul's. "It will all work out," he said. "Maybe a marriage counselor would help."

But Frank was Catholic, a sincere Catholic who believed in confession, the power of grace, and in the insolubility of marriage.

Saul dreamed that he stabbed her. Her screams tore into his flesh. The children, frightened and silent, stared at them. Their children were locked inside a prison. Then Gerda was dead, but she wasn't. She danced ahead, taunting him.

Frank was right. His research had slipped. He heard her voice in his head during the day. Lately in the privacy of his Lab, he couldn't hold back his tears. What would happen to the children if he left? He feared for them. Courageous Hannah. Darling Esther with her dark, wise eyes. When she saw him, her eyes lit up with happiness. Adam, just taking his first steps, so vulnerable and tender. It was he, Saul, who had pressured Gerda into a third pregnancy. But Adam had entered the world too late to save their marriage.

14.

A co-op bulletin flier that advertised psychic healing led Saul to Shivaya's class. *"Learn how to maintain your balance and clarity in an insane world. Discover the healing power within you."* A photograph of a young woman standing with her back arched and her arms stretched towards the sky. The flier stirred up thoughts of a legendary healer, Saul's own great-great-grandfather. Saul wrote down the phone number.

A rope to clutch before he drowned.

His first class met on a Wednesday night in an apartment with a forest green carpet. Saul was the only man among five women students. He sat in the front row on a folding chair. Shivaya, the teacher, sat very straight, her hair like a blonde helmet, her features classic Viking, and she looked at him with a frightening clarity that seemed to penetrate his being. She saw that a white hot glow surrounded him. He was emitting far more energy than the other students. He had curly black hair, brown eyes, an arresting face, a compact build. He had a certain charisma, a grounded and self-contained strength that intrigued her.

The wooden chair felt hard against his bony buttocks.

"Relax your hands, Saul," she said in her soft voice with its Danish accent. "Plant your feet firmly on the floor. Feel roots going deep into the earth. This helps to ground you so that you are totally *in* your body." He tried to imagine rope-like roots descending through the forest green carpet of her living room, down through three flights of ceilings, penetrating the concrete slab parking lot and going down still further into the molten earth's core.

"Draw earth energy up through your feet. Rich green earth energy. Draw golden energy down from the sky. Let it come down through your crown chakra and visualize that golden light energy mingling with earth energy in your solar plexus."

When he looked at her, to his embarrassment he felt himself grow hard. She was tall and slim. She wore a sundress that hung loosely over her hips. No bra. Her nipples were outlined against the pale blue fabric. Her hair gleamed under the light. Clear grey eyes. There was something in her of a medieval crusader. The large cross she might have worn over her suit of armor had been replaced by an amber pendant.

Perhaps this beautiful woman could help him manifest his own healing abilities. Perhaps he could miraculously heal Gerda! Heal their marriage! Heal their family! Heal the girls, who must be disturbed and unhappy at home. Protect the baby! Perhaps this woman could lead him to recover the power that his distant ancestor had possessed!

"Deep breaths," she said now.

All of her students, the five women and Saul, slowed their breathing. Three of the women were overweight. The fourth was anorexic. The fifth was petite and dark haired.

Shivaya surveyed her students, sat up even straighter,

and gathered her energy around her into a crystalline globe. She knew that Sharon, the dark haired one, might call her after class as she had before, her voice choked with tears because her husband was having an affair. Her psychic chords even now were pulling at Shivaya's chakras, trying to drain her strength. Yet Shivaya could not afford to let her go. As it was, she could barely pay her bills.

Shivaya's voice flowed into Saul's bones. She went to each student in turn and put her hands on their shoulders to help ground them. When she came to him, her touch sent waves of energy through his body.

He looked up at her. She smiled in a way that promised more.

"How do you feel?" she asked the students afterwards.

Sharon was weeping. Shivaya comforted her. Saul continued to "ground," mixing earth and air, earth and air with each breath. It made him feel stronger. Shivaya's hair glistened in the late afternoon light that seeped through the blinds. She knelt, caressing the woman's hands. The others sat uncomfortably, not quite knowing what to do until Shivaya straightened up and addressed them once again. Sharon wiped her eyes, calmed by Shivaya's ministrations.

"Now we will extend our auras," said Shivaya. Her eyes were brilliant and luminous.

All this flooded him as he sat on the straight-backed wooden chair and tried to bring himself back to the present, to keep himself grounded. Then she had students work in pairs to practice sending energy to each other. He had no choice but to work with one of the overweight women whose bulkiness repelled him. Afterwards Shivaya asked Saul to come to the front of the room and demonstrate on her. She felt the heat of his hands above her forehead, felt the knot of pain there melt beneath the impact of his heat.

When he returned to his chair, something about the way Shivaya looked at him seemed to penetrate some secret recess within him. As though she could see into his mind, see the pain whirling inside him and the confusion and sense of helplessness.

Childhood dreams of playing a Brahms melody on a grand piano, of rippling musical arpeggios, flooded his mind. He seemed to smell the faint perfume of Nina, long vanished. Then as he sensed Shivaya's glance, he brought himself back to the present, grounding himself through his feet, imagining that a stream of energy—a raw, reddish color—was shooting up from the center of the earth through the two floors beneath him, through the green carpet, through the soles of his leather shoes, up through his legs, through his entire body. Shivaya watched him, aware of the tumult he was experiencing, of the tears blocked in his chest over Gerda, and she knelt beside him, placing her hands gently over his. He felt strangely unlike himself.

That night, half asleep, Saul felt the presence of a spirit, a legendary great-great grandfather. You, too are a healer, said this being who looked at him with a face full of love. He felt for the warmth of Gerda's body. Her breath rose and fell rhythmically beneath the silk of her nightgown. He could feel the spirit's presence sending him strength.

15.

In the morning when she woke up, for a moment Shivaya sometimes wondered who she was, until the present came back to her and she slipped back into the enclosure of herself. The enclosure of her body, her mind, and her memories. The image of Saul came to her. What was it about him that intrigued her? For one thing, it was unusual for a man to show up at all in her classes. So many men's minds were closed to the metaphysical realm.

She took a few deep breaths, stretched in bed, unwrapped herself from the warm handmade Danish quilt, and stepped onto the carpet. Looking at herself in the mirror, she experienced an instant of satisfaction. Yes, she was slender and still beautiful at forty. Her hair gleamed golden in the sunlight.

To be alone was peaceful, although lonely at times. Telephone voices connected her to the human race. But continuous day-to-day intimacy she could not easily bear. She could not withstand people's voices and their thoughts and emotions that cut through the nerves and into her psyche.

The phone rang. Too early in the morning to answer. Too early to face other people. Ignoring its anxious ring, she poured filtered water into her kettle and put it on the stove to boil. The energy from last night's students lingered in the apartment. The image of Saul again rose. His energy was so strong. His image floated through her mind—tall, gangly, with that dark curly hair and his pale skin and glasses. There had been a stirring of sexual attraction, but he had come because he was in pain.

She toasted a slice of whole wheat bread, poured boiling water into the coffee urn with its filter, and spread cream cheese and blackberry jam on the bread. As she sipped her coffee, she leafed through the pile of bills on the table. PG&E—$53.00 for two months. Pac Bell— $27.00. Chiropractor—$43.00. Dentist—$75.00. There was never enough money. She was always slipping behind. The yoga and psychic training classes that she taught and the private readings never brought in enough.

If only she could take a regular kind of job. If, for example, she could be a sales clerk at Macy's. But she knew she would not be able to bear all those alien energies or the draining quality of the fluorescent lights.

After breakfast Shivaya did her daily meditation practice.

She visualized an aura of protection around her, protecting her from the clinging, penetrating desires of others. She visualized the clear white aura turning golden, a dark burnished gold. She visualized herself opening with clarity to produce a clear reading for the new client who would be here this afternoon for a private consultation. Even now, she could feel that woman was trying to penetrate her aura, trying to sap Shivaya's energy by sinking her psychic chords, like claws, into Shivaya's belly. That woman was a spiritual cannibal like the others.

People sought comfort in Shivaya. They found her so loving, so clear in her insights. Little did her clients know what it cost her.

A voice sounded within her at times when she was alone, and it gave her imperious commands as to how to live her life. Was this voice coming from a spirit guide or from her own inner being? She was not altogether sure. At times this voice seemed to change, to come from another consciousness.

Countless entities wafted through the air. They could haunt specific places, possess fragile psyches. At times she could feel their assaults, these greedy vampire-like spirits. Yet there must be a deeper sphere where all these divergent spirits merged into one. A sort of universal father-mother who did not err.

Unlike her own parents.

Mother: suffering martyr, tightlipped, bringing breakfast to her father and his mistress in their bed. Mother, how could you? Father, how could you? A whiff of his cologne, an image of his hawk-like features, the sound of his voice assailed her. His aristocratic lineage was tinged with a touch of syphilis. Hyper-sensitive and unbalanced, he had hurled his last words to her in anger.

Perhaps it was in an effort to understand him that Shivaya had begun to search for astrological explanations in a universe that seemed chaotic, capricious, and cruel. For years she had sought refuge in magic. With incantations and rituals she found shelter from broken love affairs, money troubles, and other torments.

So many phone calls. So many moves. Three marriages. So alone. Alone.

Now Shivaya rubbed rose oil over a white candle. Nine

o'clock on a grey November morning. She placed the candle inside its mahogany candlestick and lit it to purify the apartment. Purify with white light, with rose essence, because dangerous wisps of energy still lingered from last night's class.

Gazing into the flame, she continued her ritual. She visualized a lover coming to her. A lover who would lead her out of the wilderness of her mind, lead her out of the terrible discord produced by too many people, all wanting to take something from her, wanting to partake of her substance, strip her flesh bare, and devour even the bones.

16.

After the third class, Saul lingered as Shivaya sensed he would. She offered him a cup of tea. As he followed her into the kitchen, she was aware of how he watched the movement of her body beneath the thin cotton tunic, aware of a magnetic bond between them.

"I can't stand it anymore." His voice trembled. "I thought I could learn how to help her. But nothing helps. No visualizations. No white light."

"She doesn't want to be helped."

He was standing very close. She could smell the fear in his body and see how his nostrils flared. Gently she pushed him away, ran tap water into the kettle, and put it on the stove to boil.

"Let's go into the living room," she said.

Once there, she lit a candle, and they sat there in silence for a few moments, tranquillized by the soft light. The kettle whistled. She went into the kitchen and came back with two cups of herbal tea.

"I dream of killing her. Nightmares where I shoot her through the heart, and blood is flowing, but she keeps right on rushing towards me."

Shivaya put her hand on his. She wanted to reach out

and hold him in her arms, but she held back. She had been hurt too often in the past. And after all, he was her student. Best to observe boundaries.

She gazed at the candle flame, silent again. "Gerda's mind is not clearly hers. I see an alien force working through her. She misses a mother's love. In her loneliness and her anger, she has opened herself to something malign."

Saul hesitated, then lowered his voice. "I had an ancestor who was a famous healer."

"Saul, you are a healer, too. A strong one. But she's not ready to be helped."

"If I stay, I'm afraid I'll crack. When I come home from work, I never know what mood she'll be in. Some days she can be as sweet as gold. But too often, she yells and yells . . . and she yells at the kids . . . and I want to choke her, choke off that voice. I'm afraid of what I might do to her."

She leaned closer. She smelled of gardenias. Her shoulder brushed his. "You've got to protect yourself."

"I'm afraid for the children."

"The children will survive only if you protect yourself."

All around him he felt blackness. He had waited so long to have a family. He had wanted to be a good provider. Perhaps he had waited too long. What if he had married one of the girls in his university classes long ago, girls who looked at him with shining eyes?

Shivaya drew up her legs beneath her on the sofa, revealing a glimpse of pale thighs. "I can feel your ancestor's spirit," she said. "He is with you. He does send you strength. But Saul, you are not strong enough to stand up against her continual assaults. Something beyond herself is driving her. You need to be alone to regain your own strength."

"What about the kids? I don't want to leave them alone with her."

"They're alone with her all day while you're at work."

A shiver of electricity ran through him. Flashes of light. Flashes of a past life long ago where he had worked secretly with molten metals in an effort to turn dross into gold. Perhaps what Shivaya said about dark forces inhabiting Gerda was pure fantasy, but it rang true. Hairs rose on his flesh. In the dim candlelight, Shivaya looked soft and lovely. He held back his desire to grasp her in his arms. He needed to hold on. But he felt as if he were hanging by his fingers to the edge of a precipice.

17.

"Unless you see a psychiatrist, I'll file for divorce."

"It didn't do any good before."

"You didn't cooperate."

Gerda seethed in rage. No, this time she wouldn't blow up. She would follow through and obey like a lamb. Mind-washed lamb, mind washed of her own being. "Yes, sir," she said. "Yes, indeed."

A week later Gerda found herself in a Berkeley office with beige carpet, Venetian blinds, a worn leather couch, and a big armchair in which sat a psychiatrist with a pale, angular face and a beak-like nose. He wore a tweed jacket and dark flannel trousers. She plunked herself down on the couch opposite him. Her red high-heeled shoes pinched her toes. She wondered now why she had worn them. Certainly not to impress this nerd, his eyes shielded by thick glasses.

"I'm here under duress," she said.

He gave her an intent look. "You sound angry."

"I am. I could go on forever about my husband. He's the one who needs to be here."

"I see." He looked down at his notes.

"He's seeing some kind of crazy psychic. She sounds

like a phony, and I think it's a cover for an affair he's having with her."

He took off his glasses, wiped his face, and his expression softened. "That may well be," he said. "But let's talk about you. Tell me something about *you*. About your childhood." He flushed slightly.

Where to begin? She looked at the diplomas on the wall behind him. A barricade, she thought. Had he ever suffered, truly suffered? A jumble of emotions rose up inside her. The pink blanket. When they found her in the rubble, they let her keep the pink blanket that she had been clutching with all her might. They let her take it with her, and she slept with it. But at her aunt's and uncle's small, cluttered apartment in Berlin, it disappeared one day.

"Where is it?" she wept.

"It's a baby thing. You're not a baby anymore," said her aunt.

While they waited for papers to immigrate to the United States, she would hear her uncle and aunt argue through the thin walls of her bedroom when they thought she was asleep. "We should leave her at the orphanage," said Oncle Yosef, who had seemed kinder than her aunt. "She will be too much of a burden."

"NO!" screamed Tante Ursula. "She's my sister's child. Her father abandoned them. She's difficult, but she has no one else in the world."

Memories: There was a long scary ride on a train with low lights and the compartment crowded with smelly people. A boy with a hacking cough and a runny nose. Tante Ursula kept Gerda close against her, trying to protect her from getting sick. Cinders from the train's engine made her want to cough. Shush. She tried hard not to, and she pretended to sleep in Auntie's lap while a border guard examined their papers.

A ship. Cold and windy on deck. She remembered looking at the hypnotic grey waves and feeling the icy salt spray. Uncle was with her. Bulky in body, he was gentler than Auntie, while she was thin and scrawny with long monkey-claw fingers, too-bright blue eyes, and fading blonde hair.

So many memories. Where to begin? Words choked in her throat.

Polished oak floors in Chicago. Mahogany furniture from the Hebrew Benevolent Society. Motherly women. "Poor child." Tante Ursula would soak her feet in Epsom salts. They ached after her day-long shift at Marshall Field's. Once Tante brought her a box wrapped in blue ribbon with a new dress for special occasions. It was made of ivory taffeta, with a black velvet collar.

For months Oncle Yosef searched for work before he found a job as a security guard, a far cry from his former position as an executive with a private office. He smoked his pipe when he came home from work, just as Saul now did.

"Bad girl. Bad girl. Never touch yourself there. A bad seed."

So many memories. She talked on and on, barely conscious of all that he was saying. Floodgates bursting. Her heart pounded, and her chest hurt.

The psychiatrist looked at his watch. "Gerda, our time is up."

"But . . . I have so much more to say."

"I'll see you next Tuesday at the same time."

"I feel violated. You stirred up so much ... All week to go around with this inside is torture."

"I have patients waiting to see me."

"It's like coitus interruptus ... your stir me up ... and then leave me hanging."

"Next Tuesday at three o'clock." His face had become a barrier, as impersonal as the clock on the wall.

"Prostitute!" she screamed. "You charge for your time just like a prostitute. You feel nothing for me. I pay good money. Rather Saul does. He's the one who should be here."

"We'll talk next time."

"Fuck you!" She could barely see, she felt so angry. She took off one of her red high-heeled shoes, flung it at him, and ran out the door into the reception area, where a thin, stooped man in rimless glasses and a grey shirt sat waiting. He gave her a curious glance.

She ran back to retrieve her shoe.

The door was locked.

She screamed, "My shoe!"

The door opened a crack, and the offending shoe was flung out onto the carpet. She picked it up, put it back on, and burst out laughing. But laughter turned to tears as she got into her car.

A white hot sunlight streamed down from the sky. An aching fury inside her. She bore down on the gas. God, she was going nearly eighty. Slowed as she drove across the Bay Bridge into San Francisco. Half aware of what she was doing, she drove along the glistening waters of the Marina, up the steep slope of Broadway, and parked in an alley. She found the door of the hotel unlocked. She walked up the stairs and knocked on the German's door.

He opened it. *"Meine liebe!"* The warmth of his smile, the light in his eyes which were like her own. The warmth of his body as his arms wrapped around her. He shut the door behind them.

18.

As Saul lay on the bed on the cusp of sleep, Gerda emerged from the bathroom, naked and distraught. "I've missed my period! If I'm pregnant again, I will kill myself."

"You're not pregnant."

"How the hell do you know? You'd probably love it if we had another child. A boy! But I would go to pieces. If you were more supportive, more of a *mensch* . . . if you were more help . . . if you understood all I was going through . . . "

She went on and on, her voice pounding into him.

"Enough, Gerda!"

He walked out of the bedroom. She followed. "Damn you! Listen to me! Don't shut me up. You always do! Listen to me, damn it! . . . You're a poor excuse for a man . . . All bottled up . . . You're a failure as a husband, as a lover, and as a father. No wonder Nina jilted you! Maybe that psychic with her so-called psychic powers can teach you something!"

Her shouting had woken up the girls.

Hannah crept into Esther's bed, and they hugged each other for comfort.

"I'm sleeping with a knife under my pillow," whispered

Esther.

Adam whimpered in his sleep.

Her voice rang through the house. Saul pulled his worn overnight leather suitcase—memento of Israel—from the back of the bedroom and began to pack his neatly folded undershorts, socks, three shirts, two pairs of trousers, and his shaving implements.

"What are you doing?"

"I'm leaving."

"Get out!" she yelled. "Get the hell out!"

He strode out the front door as her voice, hurling words like venom-coated arrows, followed him. He got into his 1964 Chevy—leaving her the newer Buick—and turned on the ignition. Got into gear and backed out. Her voice still sounded in his ears through the window glass.

He drove slowly out of the driveway and onto the road. He was leaving behind him the wooded slope and the beautiful house with its reasonable mortgage and favorable location. He was leaving the scene of so much anguish. He was leaving the children. God protect them, he prayed. He envisioned auras of protection around each of them, as he had learned to do in Shivaya's class.

It might have no effect at all, he reflected, but it certainly could not hurt. Be with me now, he prayed to his distant ancestor. Give me strength. With this thought in mind he merged onto the freeway, where traffic still flowed, although it was nearly midnight.

He spent the night in a cheap motel off Highway 680, and he woke up at six A.M. A watercolor print hung on the wall opposite him. It depicted a generic blue-green meadow with pastel sky. The faint smell of disinfectant mingled with the residues of other bodies. Solitary drunks.

Furtive trysts. He showered in the narrow stall. Beneath his feet the tile floor was cold. The thin bathroom towel was wet by the time he finished drying off.

"Morning, sir. You're early today," said the security guard.

"Yes," Saul muttered. He parked in the lot closest to his Lab and went inside. Took off his windbreaker. Brewed coffee. His mind squeezed in on the project at hand, blocking out other thoughts as he manipulated glass tubing and as he meticulously mixed granules of slightly varying colors.

19.
November, 1975

Saul rented a one-bedroom apartment in North Oakland. He took only his clothing, a few books, and a few favorite music cassettes: Schubert, Brahms, Bach, Beethoven. At night when he got home from work, after a hasty dinner, he would look over the latest correspondence from his divorce attorney. Gerda was running up scary costs. With what he paid in legal fees, alimony, and child support, he had to live even more frugally than was his nature. He bought furniture from the local thrift store: a double bed, a nightstand and bureau in scarred ancient mahogany, a Formica dining table, four metal chairs, plastic plates, cups and saucers with flower motifs, and four glasses. A small black and white television completed his furnishings.

He gave himself an allowance of five hundred dollars a month. One hundred and twenty-five dollars for rent. One hundred for food. Three hundred and seventy-five for other living expenses. The remaining eight hundred were for his wife and children.

Promptly at ten o'clock on Saturday mornings he picked up Hannah and Esther, who waited for him outside the front door of their house. They carried backpacks and wore jeans, looking like hardy young adventurers.

Although it was nearly winter, it was not yet cold, and so they wore only light sweaters. Adam, who had just learned to walk, stayed with Gerda. During the day the girls would amuse themselves with board games, watch TV, or help their Dad cook and clean. Often he took them for a walk in Tilden Park. The paths stretched for miles along the coastal ridge above Berkeley. At night the girls curled up in sleeping bags and slept on the shag carpet. At times their noisy laughter and constant chatter caused him raging migraines, and he would retire to the darkness of his bedroom. He began to understand the strains that Gerda had felt.

She left angry phone messages at the Lab. He received the pink message slips from secretaries who smiled with smug commiseration. She threatened to kill the children if he were even a day late with child support. Although he believed that she would never follow through, a constant underlying fear plagued him. Despite everything, she loved the children, he told himself. Yes, she loved them. She needed them. A Jewish mother's sacred right.

He immersed himself in his experiments in the Lab. Whenever he discovered a new method or an unexpected result, he felt elated. At night he frequently dreamed about his work and woke up with fresh ideas.

Most evenings he hastily cooked a hamburger along with Birds Eye peas, and he brewed a cup of chamomile tea, which Shivaya had suggested for relaxation. Barely tasting the food, he watched the evening news. The screen dissolved into a blurred mix of background sound and images. Memories of his German childhood filtered back. Always there had been the smell of something fresh-baked. Cabbage rolls or strudel or cake. On Friday nights there was *challah.* Always a hot meal. Split pea or lentil soup. On special occasions, brisket with cabbage. Women would hover over the dining table. His frail ninety-year-old grandmother sat in a corner. She refused to eat before the family had finished, in order to make sure there was enough for everyone else, and she consumed only leftover fatty meat. Nonetheless, she practically outlived them all! She had died just before the family left Germany. There had been his mother with her smug manner, which so infuriated him. There had also been his elderly, white-haired Aunt Deborah, who would quietly slip him an occasional bar of chocolate as a token of her love.

In the evening he would sit down at the kitchen table with his brother, sister, and father, while the women served them. After a short prayer led by his father—except for Friday nights when his mother lit the Shabbat candles with her own special prayer—they ate quickly, not lingering, because there was much to be done—studying, more cooking, and cleaning up. After the homework was finished, perhaps he would play a game of chess with his father. Life was orderly and predictable. As solid as their mahogany furniture, before the times changed and before stability began to slip away with the advent of Hitler Youths and increasing edicts against Jews.

Before someone painted a crude yellow star on the door of the local tailor's shop. That had been a symbol to the *goyim* to boycott, or worse, to vandalize. A week before *Kristallnacht,* someone hurled a brick through his father's laboratory window. On that night, his father's laboratory burned to the ground.

20.

"Good riddance," she yelled when Saul drove his Chevy out of the driveway into the dark night. Afterwards she collapsed on the living room carpet and wept. Adam, who had managed to climb out of his crib, crawled into her arms after taking a few uncertain steps. "Ma . . . Mama . . . ma," he crooned. He patted her face with his pudgy fingers. *My baby! My love! He loves me!* Tiny creature with Saul's dark hair.

The girls, still in their pajamas, also crept up to her. Hannah kissed her cheek. Esther stroked her shoulders. "It's okay, Mom," Esther murmured in a rare expression of tenderness. "We love you."

For three days Gerda did not shower or brush her teeth or eat anything except dry cornflakes. On the third day she opened his closet to see what remained. Empty except for a frayed white cotton shirt from Goodwill. Saving money was his thing. Why pay fifteen dollars, he said, when he could get one for fifty cents? He had taken the good tweed jacket and flannel trousers that she had bought for him at Macy's. While he professed a total lack of interest in clothing, he depended on her.

She drank what was left of the scotch and swallowed a

strong sleeping pill at night. How would she survive? Only twenty dollars and nineteen cents in her purse. There was $1,000 in their checking account, which Saul always kept there to avoid check charges, and a savings account for which only he had the card. She stayed in her nightgown, her feet bare.

Please let my period come, she begged her body. Shed lots of blood. Shed this fetus, if it's there. I can't handle being pregnant. I will die whether it's Saul's or the German's. I can't bear it.

At night Hannah and Esther crept into her bed and tried to comfort her. She caressed them and wept. "I love you," she sobbed. "Forgive all the terrible things I've done. I love you."

They fed and clothed Adam and played with him and didn't go to school. Adam learned to speak a few more words, and they read to him from picture books. He thrived with all the extra attention.

On the third morning the phone rang. It was Saul. "Are you all right?" he asked. She was silent. "Do you want me to come back?"

"No," she hissed. "No. But one day I might strangle your kids."

"No, you won't!" cried Hannah. The girl seemed so far away. Everyone seemed distant. She was in a dream: loving them and then hating them all moments later. Who was she? The monster who abused them? The woman who loved them? She was in a dream.

Four days later the girls resumed going to school. Alone in the house with Adam, Gerda stood in the kitchen, barefoot and in her robe. The sun beamed strong light through the kitchen curtains. She picked up the phone with a shaky hand and phoned Barbara. "The neighbors used to give me strange looks," she said. "What will they think of me now? They see Saul as the good guy. The saint."

"Well, he's no saint," said Barbara, her voice strong and husky. "And you are crazy!" She laughed. "You and me, we're both crazy! Two of a kind! That's why we're friends!" She sounded drunk from the effects of wine, although it was only ten in the morning.

"I don't know what I'm going to do."

"You'll survive. You're tough."

"What if I'm pregnant?"

"Weren't you taking precautions?"

"Well . . . there was one time . . . " Her voice faltered. "I could be pregnant. I don't know yet."

"If you are, then ask for more child support."

"I can't bear to think about it!" she moaned. She couldn't tell Barbara the truth. What if the fetus inside her—if there were one—what if it were the German's? It could only be his! She and the German made love just once, after the fiasco with the shrink. But it took only one sperm, smaller than the smallest speck of dust, to connect with an egg, to create a new life, and to destroy hers.

"Gerda, when could you have gotten pregnant?"

"I could have gotten off rhythm with my pills," Gerda muttered. In truth, she had recently been depending on a diaphragm, as the birth control pills caused her bloating and discomfort.

"I gotta go," she said in a rush. "Adam's hungry."

"Love you, honey. Take care of yourself! Congratulations on kicking the bastard out! I never did like him!"

Barbara's warm voice. Yet she was treacherous.

Gerda slammed down the phone, bit her lips, and wanted to cry again.

She sank down at the kitchen table, her head in her hands. After a while she looked up and gazed through the window at the deck, which was bordered with the spruce and laurel trees they had planted years ago when she and Saul first moved in. Finally she stood up, showered for the first time since Saul's departure, and dressed in slacks and a heavy, shapeless sweater. It was chilly November weather. She bundled up Adam in warm clothing and drove with him to the Safeway for groceries.

That afternoon, while the girls were still at school, she stood over Adam as he napped in his crib. She had a faraway look in her eyes. Seed of Saul. Saul's hair. Saul's skin. So easy to kill. Shake him hard. Bludgeon him. Stab him with a kitchen knife. So many ways to kill.

As if sensing her thoughts, he stirred in his sleep. She lifted him up from the crib. He struggled to free himself and began to cry. She set him down on the changing table. His diaper was soaking wet. She flung the horrid wet diaper into the pail. Then she washed and powdered him. His little penis. Tiny rosebud head. All hers. His body. All hers. Fresh clean diaper.

His downy hair like Saul's. His eyes, blue like her own. His face was red, swollen, and wet with tears. (Kiss the little penis or snip it off?) He gave a loud piercing scream. "Quiet!" she hissed. Her voice frightened him. His cries subsided. She rocked him gently in her arms, then put him down again. He seemed to understand, because after she left his room, which they had painted a cheery yellow with large duck and sheep decals, he rocked himself silently, thoughtfully within the confines of his crib.

Blood began to flow between her thighs.

She sank down on the floor and wept with relief.

21.

Saul loved the Greek tavern in Berkeley where on weekends musicians played and crowds filled the large room with its wooden floor and dim lighting. He loved the rhythm of Greek dances. He loved structured steps. In folk dance groups he felt safe in a way he did not feel when he was alone. Something stirred in his blood, something ancient, older than the Jewish rituals he had learned as a child, something primitive and earthy and good. He loved to lead line dances, and he loved to improvise when he was in the center of the circle. Each improviser would dance a few steps and then hand the sweaty red handkerchief he was holding to the next dancer.

One night in March he met a girl no older than thirty, a beautiful girl with long chestnut hair and green cat's eyes and creamy skin who wore a blue skirt that flared around her legs and a white blouse that fell off her shoulders, a girl with curving breasts and an alluring glance. She invited him home afterwards.

The girl lived in a fringe neighborhood in an older frame house, not too far from the Greek tavern. Several junked cars were parked in the next yard. Her living room was filled with plants, and there was an odor of patchouli.

She offered him a joint, put on some Rolling Stones music, and time passed more slowly. How beautiful her skin was, how soft, and when he caressed her shoulders, she moved closer and kissed him on the lips.

Later they ended up in her bed, and they made love. Then, as he drove back to his apartment, he began to feel very depressed. That night he dreamed he was surrounded by thick stone walls. In his hand he held a glittering diamond. If he threw the diamond over the walls, he would be free. He threw it, but then he found himself wandering through a dark maze.

He woke up with a flat feeling. In all the years of his marriage, he had been faithful. Now, although they were separated, he felt he had betrayed Gerda. He had betrayed his marriage vows with this shallow sexual act. Why had he not loved Gerda in the way she needed to be loved? If he had loved her—truly loved her—then perhaps all would have been different. He had let himself slip in a way that threatened the entire structure of his life. He thought of the cyanide stored in his Lab. He could compress a bit of the powder into a pill—they sold gelatin capsules at the co-op pharmacy. He would somehow have to make the death look accidental. Then Gerda and the children could at least get his insurance money. Gerda was always screaming that they did not have enough—that the children lacked decent clothes—that Adam would soon need nursery school. If he were dead, Gerda could begin a new life. Perhaps marry again. As a wealthy widow she would be more likely to attract a husband than as a struggling divorcée.

Saul wanted the comfort of shedding tears, but he felt drained and dry. He tried to swallow a bit of toast, and he couldn't. He took a small sip of coffee. It was Saturday morning. Get ready to pick up the girls.

22.

It began for Hannah during the winter of eighth grade. The artificial feeling. *I am not acting real,* she would think. *I am not real. I don't exist,* pressed between my mother's and father's spirits, suffocated by their warring. While she responded cheerily to her friends' overtures, she felt as if she were artificial, a windup doll.

Mornings of her mother screaming at her. *I have sacrificed my life for you children. You damn well owe me something. It is because of you that Saul left me!* Lonely in the house without Dad. Mother was scary, too. The look in her eyes sometimes.

"You are my life, Hannah! I would die for you!"

"Then don't be mean, Mom. Don't hit me, and tell me I'm bad. Don't come after me with a knife!"

Hannah wanted to vomit this alien being inside her, the being that would choke little Adam, choke and stab everyone inside the house, stab Dad in the heart.

They don't like me, she thought. My friends only pretend to like me. They pretend, just the way I am pretending to be normal.

Her body was changing. Blood every month now. The curse, her mother called it, and when she told her mother about the blood, her mother lightly slapped her across both cheeks. It was the custom, she said. She told her younger sister Esther about it, hoping to prepare Esther so she would be spared the shock and shame she herself had felt.

Now there was pubic hair, and she had breasts with nipples that stuck out like miniature erect penises, and with the change in her body came increased sensitivity, as though a protective covering, a psychic skin had been peeled off.

Everything brought pain and wonderment.

She began writing poetry.

"It's beautiful," said Gerda in one of her calm and loving moments. "Your poetry is beautiful."

Sometimes she thought her mother was thinking through her, and her thoughts and feelings did not seem to belong to herself at all. At other times she heard her father's voice. "No, I can't make things all right," he would say to Gerda. Cold, compressed, unable to reach out to her mother, he would walk away, and that father-being was also inside her.

"I love you the most of all my children. You are the most like me. Oh, I am lonely, my darling child. You are a friend to me, not just a daughter." Gerda nestled her chin against Hannah's soft dark hair. At that instant her mother's force flowed into Hannah.

Later Hannah vomited, but she could not get it out.

It lodged there.

She could not get it out.

Maybe she could kill herself because it would be less painful to be dead, to be floating around somewhere as a disembodied being. No homework. No anxiety about whether people liked her. No more fear. No more wondering what to do with her long unruly hair. No more homework pressure. No more worry. No more pain.

On a visit to Saul's for the weekend, she screamed over and over again, "I hate you, Daddy. You bastard!" as she lay down on the carpet and pounded her fists against the shag fabric.

Later she could not imagine why she had become so angry. She could not remember what he had done to arouse her rage.

"I hate you, Daddy Bastard."

"I love you the most. You are the closest to me of my children." The voice of her mother. speaking through her. *"He destroyed me. Get even with that bastard for me. Get revenge."*

Hannah began vomiting at night, but Gerda's voice stayed lodged within her, while her father's very being filled her with rage. The set of his jaw and the cast of his dark eyes were like her own.

"He drove me crazy," her mother sobbed one day. She was lying in bed, a damp wash cloth over her forehead for her headache, while Hannah perched on the edge of the bed. *"I was okay before I married him. In Chicago I had friends I'd known since first grade. I felt at home there. But he took and took. Hannah, he never gave. He took my youth. He drained me. I could have been an actress. I could have been someone. I did not sign up for this life. I sacrificed what I could have been for you children."*

While she both pitied and raged against her mother, at times she felt more like her father.

He was silent and stubborn.

She would be more silent and more stubborn.

She would beat him at his own game.

23.

One rainy night Saul appeared at Shivaya's door. He looked haggard, and there were bags under his eyes. "I had to leave her," he blurted out. "Otherwise, I'd have killed her." Still standing in the doorway, he lurched towards her. His trench coat was slick with rain. She could smell alcohol on his breath, and she drew back.

"Shivaya, help me!"

"Come inside. You're drenched. I'll make you a cup of tea."

He followed her into the kitchen. "I need something stronger."

"Okay." Her voice was husky. He'd already had quite a bit to drink, which was not like him, she reflected. Nonetheless, she took a nearly empty bottle of Courvoisier out of the cupboard and poured its remaining contents into a glass.

He gulped down the liquor.

"I worry constantly about the kids. It's hard leaving them alone with her."

"Of course it's hard, Saul. But you have to survive."

He gazed at her intently. "You're beautiful. I want to hold you in my arms."

She flinched. "It's best we keep a distance. You're my student, after all."

"I'm falling in love with you."

She looked into his eyes. They were dark and gentle.

To be loved by him. If only she could sink into it, like sinking into eiderdown, but danger flashed. Red light. Sobs in the dark. Shades of knife thrusts to the heart.

"Look for someone else," she said. "I'm not the one for you."

"It's you I want."

There was strength beneath his voice that drew her to him, in spite of herself.

He clasped her against him. His heat filled her body. She felt herself melting. "No," she said. She pushed him away, resisting her desire to sink into his embrace. "Go," she said. "Just go."

A week later she accepted his dinner invitation. He took her to a Thai restaurant, an intimate place with soft lighting. Dinner was rich coconut curry soup, creamy with tart lemongrass and slices of coconut and red peppers. Barbequed chicken with sweet-sour sauce, roasted zucchini, rice, and fragrant tea.

Shivaya talked about her childhood. "My father left when I was only five," she said. "He was a poet. An eccentric, brilliant man. He treated my mother terribly. She left him, then remarried. I desperately wanted a father. I used to hide behind the front door in the evening while I waited for my stepfather to come home from work. He was a cold man. I would whisper, 'Daddy,' rehearsing how I would say it, but then the words would stick my throat."

Warmed by a glass of strong sake, Saul leaned over the

table, took her hands in his, and kissed her. A long kiss. Their lips felt so warm against each other. Saul's tongue moved inside her mouth.

He took her dancing at the Greek tavern. She watched him lead a plump raven-haired woman in a circle, his left arm wrapped around her shoulder, his right arm wrapped just below her breast. At that moment she imagined him two thousand years ago as the pasha of a harem in the Middle East.

Long after they became lovers, she felt as if he had woven an invisible net around her. He thrust chords of owning into all her chakras. He offered financial help. He loaned her $1,000, to be paid off at some indefinite time or simply written off as a bad debt.

After sex, whether or not she had experienced an orgasm, her third eye opened like a golden flower. Energy shot up from her vagina through her body to the third eye inside her skull. The comfort of him. The warmth of his body against hers. They gave each other some sort of primal comfort.

While she soared in her spirit, he provided an anchor. Although his imagination was limited, beneath the surface of his words lay a vast sea of spirit. It was this that drew her. But over time it could render her parasitic if she let him get too close.

24.
April, 1976

Hannah lay on the roof. The rough pebbles and tar scratched her body. She watched the people below: her mother and three policemen. A branch from the maple tree waved in the wind and blew close to her face. Through the green budding leaves she watched them, feeling as distant as if she were light years away, as if she were watching them through a kaleidoscope, blobs of shifting color and form.

For hours she had lain on the roof, and the sun was beginning to sink beneath the horizon. She heard voices and peered further over the edge. Her mother and two policemen emerged from the house. They were right beneath her. If she threw a pebble down, it would hit them.

"I don't know where she is," Gerda said in her sharp, cutting voice. "This morning we had a tiff—nothing much—I just want her to be okay." She broke into a sob. "It's hard," she cried. "It's so hard."

Hannah wanted to howl with glee. She gloated, but the sadness was inside her. She wanted to cry. *Gotcha, Mom. You were chasing me with a butcher knife. Gotcha now for all those times you hit us and screamed at us. Told us we were bad. Told us it was all our fault that Dad left.*

"We are so alike," sobbed Gerda below. Her voice grew softer. "She is the one closest to me."

Her sister Esther would go limp like a rag doll, willing herself to show no emotion, while Hannah would scream back. "Hannah, you're the one with guts," her father, Saul, would say.

One of the policemen was filling out a report. *What does she look like? Medium height—about five feet three— fourteen years old—nearly fifteen. Long wavy black hair. Birthmarks? Other marks of identification just in case she turned up in a hospital or worse?* Finally they left. She watched them get into their car, and she crawled over to the other side of the roof so she could watch them drive off. Then she crawled back to watch her mother pace back and forth along the deck. Saw her mother go inside the house. Now Gerda would be on the phone, calling her friends, and everyone would be frantic. Good! Dad would be upset, too. Good! Let him suffer!

Why did you leave us?

Much later, after a thin sliver of moon had risen in the night sky, she realized she was hungry. She was beyond hungry. She felt light and spacey as she climbed down from the roof. When she got to the ground, she tightened the laces of her sneakers and walked along the dark street, past the neat suburban houses with their shrubbery and trees, towards the center of town and then into a coffee shop. She watched the people. There was gangly red-haired Andrew from her class with his Dad. It hurt her to watch them together along with his yucky mother, who was smiling at the two of them.

"Can I have a glass of water?" she asked the pimply-faced clerk behind the counter.

"Sure, sweetheart. Anything else?"

"No thanks."

As he handed her the water, their fingers touched briefly. "What are you doing out so late all alone?"

Andrew and his parents glanced over at her from their table.

What a jerk! "None of your fucking business."

She walked out the door, slowly sipping the water in its cardboard cup. Where could she get something to eat? She walked and walked until the street she was on gave way to a dirt road. Walked up a hill. And there just on the other side was her friend Jeanie's house. Several cars were parked outside, along with rusted wrecks of cars, a car engine, a cast-off refrigerator. A dog chained to a post barked as she approached. "Hey, cool it, Smokey," she said in a calm voice.

She had learned to act calm, to speak calmly when inside it was a tornado, a flood, an earthquake all combined. The dog recognized her. Slowly she came up to him and patted his neck. He began wagging his tail furiously, licking her fingers. "Nice Smokey," she crooned. "You're a decent dog."

A fat, dark-haired man in stained work clothes appeared on the porch. "Who's there?"

"Hannah."

"Come on in, honey,"

He had been drinking, she could tell from the way his breath smelled, and his hand on her shoulder gave her a sense of unease.

"Where's Jeanie?"

"She's upstairs."

"I'll go up and see her."

"Hey, just a minute . . . " His voice, drunken and slurred, gave her the shivers. Where the hell was Jeanie's mother? She was usually around, a pale, frightened creature. Hannah heard more men's voices from the living room. The sound of a game on television. She ran quickly up the wooden stairs and along the narrow hallway to Jeanie's room, pounded on the door, and walked in without waiting for anyone to open it.

Jeanie and her sister Maureen were lounging on the twin beds.

"Trouble with your Mom?" asked Jeanie.

"Yeah."

Maureen was painting her toenails bright magenta. Music was playing on the stereo. Books were spread open on Jeanie's bed. "I'm doing my math," she said. "You can help me."

"Okay," said Hannah, glad of a task to do. "But first I need to eat something. I'm starving."

Jeanie handed her a half-empty bag of potato chips. "Help yourself."

"Is that all you've got?"

"Yeah . . . We can go down to the kitchen . . . but later."

"Okay," said Hannah, understanding all too well that neither of them wanted to tangle with her Dad or his friends.

"I hope they don't stay too long. Where's your Mom?"

"Sleeping."

"With that racket downstairs?"

"Yeah. She's tired."

For a while they worked on algebra problems, lounging on Jeanie's bed with its white chenille spread. Hannah lay on her stomach and burrowed against the mattress, right against Jeanie's shoulder and arm. Jeanie smelled slightly of vanilla soap. Hannah scratched numbers on a pad of paper with a ballpoint pen that spurted uneven squiggles of ink. A bit smudged on the spread.

"Oh, I'm sorry," said Hannah. She went into the adjoining bathroom for a sponge to wash off the stain. The bathroom was littered with damp towels. A roll of wet toilet paper sat on top of the tank. There was none in the holder. In contrast to Jeanie's clean scent, the room stank of mold and wet towels. Lipsticks and other cosmetics littered the counter. She found a rag beneath the sink, wet it, and tried to clean off the ink stain on the bedspread, but it remained.

"Oh, never mind," said Jeanie. She stood up and stretched. Jeanie was shorter than Hannah and very skinny, with freckles and auburn hair that cascaded over her shoulders. Very fair skin and green eyes. She was wearing a white T-shirt and panties printed with small red hearts. She was popular in school. Inside the clique to which she granted Hannah entrée, the clique that Hannah frequented on the outer edges.

"I'm tired. I'm going to sleep," she said. She went into the bathroom to brush her teeth and wash up, while Hannah put away the books on the bed, took off her jeans, and stretched out under the covers.

The floor creaked. Wind rose, and it blew branches against the window. The voices downstairs died down. It was dark all through the house. Jeanie lay next to her, breathing softly in her sleep, her warm skin touching Hannah. Soft warm body next to her, cuddle against Jeanie. She turned and lay on her side, put her arms around Jeanie for comfort. Jeanie barely stirred.

Steps in the hallway. Door opening. If Jeanie's Dad came inside, she would scream. Scream and scream. Slowly the door closed. The steps receded along the hallway. Hannah heard him piss in the bathroom, heard the toilet flush, heard something drop, and heard him curse. Her body tensed. Jeanie's breathing grew more troubled. She rolled away from Hannah.

Hannah held her breath. Slowly the noises quieted down. Jeanie's breathing resumed its natural rhythm. Hannah pressed against Jeanie's body for warm comfort, and finally she slept a little.

"Are you coming to school?" Jeanie asked in the morning.

"No."

"What will you do?"

"I don't know."

The girls dressed. Jeanie put her books into her backpack, and they went down into the kitchen, which was littered with empty beer bottles, cigarette butts, dirty dishes, and the lingering trace of marijuana. In the refrigerator there was white bread, peanut butter, and a half-empty jar of grape jelly. They made sandwiches and heated up instant coffee. Jeanie cut an orange, hard with age, into slices. Everyone else in the house was still asleep. But just as they were leaving the house, Jeanie's mother appeared, a frail, slightly hunched figure in a faded blue bathrobe, hastily tied, her hair mouse-colored and straggly. Her face looked pasty. Her eyes, however, were dark, intense, and alive.

"Have a good day, girls," she said. She looked in dismay at the dishes and began to putter around the kitchen.

Hannah parted from Jeanie where the dirt road gave way to concrete paving. While Jeanie walked towards school, Hannah turned onto the path that led to a bike trail. Where was she going? She didn't know. A large black bird circled above her, then soared higher and disappeared from view.

25.

One morning when Shivaya woke up, she decided that she must get away. Everything was oppressive. The walls of her apartment. The smell of bacon and fried potatoes from an apartment downstairs. They must be cooking with the door wide open.

Unpaid bills beckoned from her desk. PG&E—$14.83. Pac Bell—$49.90. How had she spent so much on the phone? Ah yes, phoning her sister in Copenhagen. Phoning her old friend Ingrid who now lived in San Diego. Perhaps she should move there. Better climate. Beaches. Ocean. Close to Mexico. Being near a border—close to escape if necessary—was intriguing.

The phone rang. Again and again. An insistent ring. Reluctantly she picked it up.

"Hannah is missing." Saul's voice, mournful and somehow accusing.

"What happened?"

"I don't know. Probably a fight with her mother."

"How long has she been gone?"

"Since yesterday."

Shivaya was silent for a moment.

"Saul, I feel she's okay."

"How do you know?"

"After you spoke, I would have felt it if anything bad had happened to her. She's safe for now. I will visualize golden light around her, protective light. You can do that, Saul, too."

"The police are looking for her."

"They won't find her. She'll come back when she's ready. Just keep visualizing her safe; visualize light around her; visualize a protective aura of golden light."

"Shivaya, I need to see you."

"Not now, Saul. It won't help. I was practically out the door when you called. I'm going away for a couple of days."

"Where?"

"Down the coast."

"When will you be back?"

"In a few days. Saul, I've got to get away. I need to rest. People have drained my energy. Can you understand?"

"Yes," he said. "Do what suits you." His voice was cold.

After she hung up, his heaviness lingered. She had seen a photo of Hannah, and she sat for a few minutes quite still until she glimpsed an image of the girl wandering along a path in the woods. She mentally projected a diaphanous wall of protection around the girl.

As she showered, she tried to clear herself of alien energy, all these people clutching at her survival chakras. Especially Saul with his heaviness, his guilt-tripping vibe. She put on jeans, tank top, sandals. Made coffee. Heated up a bran muffin. Spooned yoghurt and blackberries into a bowl. How much did she have in her checking account? Eighty-one dollars. Her students paid on the first of the month, which was two weeks away. She owed over $5,000 on her credit card, and she'd been pulling in only enough to cover her rent and groceries, each month going deeper into debt. She could ask Saul for a loan if she absolutely had to, but she didn't want to do that.

She tried so hard. Why was it so difficult for her, always so difficult? Fog around her brain. After coffee, the fog cleared a bit. She packed a few things into her canvas overnight bag, got into her van, and drove south on Interstate 80 until she hit the 101. Took the Santa Cruz turnoff. Drove up through the mountains and descended along steep winding roads until she hit the ocean.

A few hours later she was lying on the sand. It felt soft beneath her body. The sun warmed her back, burning her bare buttocks, which were paler than the rest of her body, covered as they had been by bathing suit bottoms. But now she was naked. It felt so good. The grains of sand against her skin. She burrowed deeper into the soft white sand. Sound of waves crashing. A dog trotted along the beach. She raised her head and watched it move towards her. It approached, sniffed her, and shook water from its wet fur.

"Get away, dog!" She rose, attempting to shoo the creature away. Just then a human figure in hooded sweatshirt and long pants appeared in the distance. Male or female? The wind blew against her, chilling her. There was a loud whistle, and the dog bounded back towards its owner.

Shivaya picked up her towel and beach things and moved to the shelter of the dunes.

Stretched out again on her stomach and watched the figure walk past, the dog trotting beside it. They receded into the distance. No one else was on the beach. She turned over onto her back and let the sun warm her. Put on a thin film of lotion. She was getting tan all over, but her breasts and lower belly were reddish with burn. She smoothed more lotion on them. Surveyed the beach.

No one was in sight.

She rose and walked into the surf. Icy cold. Like the seashore where they used to vacation when she was a child. Memories of that seaside village flitted through her mind: the blackberry brambles, her first kiss with a boy from the village. Her fingers and toes were turning blue, numb. After a few moments she came out of the water. Ah, it was so fresh. So good. Lying in the sand, letting the sun dry her, she felt strengthened, invigorated by the fresh salt smell in the air, the breeze, the sound of the surf, rhythmic, soothing.

That night she camped on a beach a few miles south of Santa Cruz. She had brought a small tent, along with her sleeping bag and a ground cloth. Two or three other tents were pitched along the dunes. She felt safer camping near a few other people, but not too close. They were several hundred yards away. She looked up at the stars. So beautiful. So much more visible here than in the smoggy air of the East Bay.

Sleep, murmured the Mother Goddess.

At dawn she took a quick dip in the icy water, dried herself off, put on jeans and a sweatshirt, and packed her things in the trunk of her car. Walked barefoot along the beach and watched the sun rise. "Red sky in the morning, sailors take warning." But there was no red sky, and there was just a beautiful pale pink tinge along the edge of the dark horizon. Gradually the sky lightened. She was chilly, and to warm herself she began to run. Ran and ran along the soft sand, keys jingling in her pocket.

26.

On her way back from Santa Cruz, Shivaya stopped at the Safeway to pick up some groceries. As she was driving out of the parking lot, she saw a girl with long dark hair walking in front of her. The ragged edges of her jeans trailed the pavement. Her gaze was downwards, and she exuded fear. With a slight shock, Shivaya realized that the girl was Saul's oldest daughter, Hannah, the troubled one, the adventurous one who seemed to take all the family discord into herself.

She slowed down alongside the girl and stopped, opened the window and called out the girl's name.

The girl kept on walking, as if she hadn't heard.

"You're Saul's daughter, aren't you?"

The girl walked faster.

Shivaya slid the key out of the ignition, opened the door, and ran after her.

"Your father's been so worried about you!"

"He should be," the girl muttered. She kept on walking.

Shivaya overtook her. "Please," she said, slightly out of breath. "Listen to me. I can help you."

"How do you know my father?"

"He takes classes with me."

"I've heard about you." The girl halted in her tracks and gave her a hostile look. "Mom says you're the reason he left us."

"I had nothing to do with it."

"What do you want with me?"

"I know you're afraid of going home."

The girl shuddered. "Just leave me alone." She continued walking.

"It will go easier with your Mom if I'm with you."

"My Mom hates you!"

"Even if she does, it will be easier if I'm there. Come on, I'll give you a ride."

"What are you getting out of this?" Hannah looked her full in the face, and beneath the bold hostility, Shivaya perceived an immense longing for tenderness.

"I don't know," Shivaya said in a soft voice. "I know your father loves you very much, and . . . I feel connected to you somehow. I ran away when I was your age."

"Really?"

"Yes, I did. I'll tell you about it someday. Come on, let me drive you home."

After a moment's hesitation, Hannah said, "Okay. Whatever," in a resigned voice, as if she had given up all hope of anything, and slowly she walked back with Shivaya to the van. When Shivaya opened the passenger door, Hannah hesitated once more, then got in. The van smelled of salt air from the sea, and the worn leather seat felt grainy with sand.

"I'm sorry about the sand. I was at the ocean," Shivaya remarked.

"I love the ocean."

Shivaya felt a surge of empathy. *Maybe I can take her*

there one day. Breathe deeply in and out. Send her light. Ground both of us. The girl is beautiful, and she's brave. But she's been so fucked over. Saul, why couldn't you protect her.

Before they got out, Shivaya took a business card out of her purse and handed it to the girl. "Call me," she said, "If you feel like it."

Gerda heard car tires crunch against the gravel. When she looked out the living room window she saw Hannah and a blonde woman get out of the car. She recognized Shivaya from the photo on the fliers that advertised her classes. A fake holy woman! Saul's whore! She'd heard about their affair. Thank God, Hannah was safe. But why was she bringing that woman here?

She looked down at her shirt. It had a dried food stain on it where Adam had spilled egg. It was a large work shirt she'd worn during pregnancy. Now she'd gained so much weight that it hid her body, covering the elastic-waist jeans.

The blonde whore was so slender and tanned. Oh, she hated her.

Hannah opened the door, and the two of them stood at the threshold. Gerda got up, went to the door, and just stood there for a moment, very still. She gave the whore a murderous look.

"What are you doing with Hannah?" Her voice was slurred; she smelled of liquor.

"I gave her a lift."

"Come in," she finally said.

"We need to talk," said Shivaya in a low voice.

They sat down at the kitchen table. Gerda took a swig from the bottle of scotch that stood before her.

"Hannah, *where were you?*"

"I ran away because I was scared of you, Mom."

"I've been through hell. I didn't know if you were alive or dead."

Turning to Shivaya, she said, "I want you to know I would do anything for Hannah. I would die for her."

"Then why don't you live for me, Mom, and straighten out your life?" cried Hannah.

"I love Hannah. I would never hurt her."

"Liar! You've said you wanted to kill us."

"I was overwhelmed. I never meant it."

"You sure sounded like you meant it all those times you've threatened Dad over the phone. Sometimes you get crazy, and then I'm really scared."

"That's absurd! You know I would never hurt you."

"You already have hurt me. In a lot of ways, Mom. Why not face up to what you've done?"

There was a tense silence. Gerda's eyes narrowed in anger as she again surveyed Shivaya in her white tank top that revealed the shapes of her nipples.

What have you got, whore, that I lack?

Hidden inside the bedroom, Esther was listening. She wanted to scream as she heard their loud voices. Hannah got all the attention. She, Esther, was the invisible one. She deliberately kept quiet, in order to avoid injury. She went into Adam's room. He had awakened from his afternoon nap, and he was attempting to climb out of his crib. She lifted him over the rail and set him down on the floor, where he toddled over to a pile of toys on the rug and picked out a red truck. "Where's the truck going?" she asked.

"Fire!" he cried. "Fire!" He got down on hands and

knees and zoomed the truck across the floor.

Shivaya heard the children in the next room, but she focused on the pain and confusion in Gerda's eyes. The woman was frail. Underneath Gerda the bully lay a frightened child.

I must be gentle with her, she thought. So gentle.

Shivaya lit a cigarette—an elegant Swedish brand that she rarely smoked—and offered one to Gerda, but Gerda shook her head in refusal.

They heard a crash in Adam's room, and he began to wail.

"I'm going to see Adam," said Hannah.

Esther appeared in the doorway. Hannah ran over to her sister and hugged her. The two girls then rushed to attend to Adam.

Gerda hunched over the table, her head in her hands. "I get overwhelmed," she said. "There's no one here for me." Her voice caught in a sob.

"I'm sorry." Shivaya reached out for her hand, but Gerda pulled away.

"Maybe you can clue me in." Gerda's voice rose in emotion. "You're the reason he left. You're fucking him. I know that. What's your secret? How much do you charge?" Her shirt, partially unbuttoned, exposed her full breasts as she leaned towards Shivaya.

"He's suffering," said Shivaya, who had stiffened with tension. "He pays what the other students do. Six dollars a class." She fought her impulse to leave immediately, but she knew she had to stay awhile and try to calm this woman or it would go badly for the girl.

Gerda's face crumpled. Her eyes watered with tears. "What is it in me he cannot love?"

Shivaya felt the full force of the woman's desperation, and her heart filled with pity. She tried to send waves of calming light.

"He began coming to my classes," said Shivaya, "because he wanted to save the marriage. He wanted you to come to the classes, too."

"Really? I don't think so," murmured Gerda.

She lifted her gaze. There were bags under her eyes from lack of sleep, and her skin was beginning to show the traces of age. Aquiline features, full lips, thin brows. Her eyes held such sadness. Such deep sadness. Lifetimes of sadness.

"There's no one. No one's here for me."

"You have the children. You're a mother," Shivaya said softly.

"Without a mate."

Gerda poured herself another shot of scotch.

"Hannah knows you love her."

"I've been a bad mother."

"You did the best you could."

Suddenly Gerda's face twisted into anger, and flames streamed against the dark grey cloud that had surrounded her. "You're his whore!"

Shivaya's voice quivered. "It's not about fucking. Marriage is a lot more than that."

"He never would have left if it weren't for you."

"Who knows," said Shivaya quietly. "Fate is what it is."

Gerda sat still, lost in thought. "Hannah ran away. I love her the most, and she left me."

"She was scared."

"Damn her!"

Shivaya's heart pounded. She continued to send the woman waves of light.

A burst of wind blew against the curtains, and Shivaya shivered with cold. The anger left Gerda's body, and she burst into heartrending sobs. "I love her the most," she repeated. "Hannah is the only one who understands me at all. I would die for her."

Shivaya folded Gerda in her arms and caressed her gently, as if she were a child.

"You've done the best you could," Shivaya murmured. "Hannah knows you love her. I know she loves you, too."

As she stroked the woman's back and shoulders, holding her close, Gerda's sobs gradually subsided, and she drew back, sat up, and seemed lost in thought.

It was Saul who drove me crazy, thought Gerda. I didn't use to be this way. Where I needed hard resistance—a strong male voice, someone to hold me when hysteria gripped me—where I wanted response and warmth— there was nothing. Rather there was a cold, angry voice.

Saul used to come home from work and dump his briefcase by the front door. "Saul," I might say in a light-hearted tone. "It's cocktail hour. Let's have a drink."

Sometimes I was already a little tipsy.

"Let me be," he would say.

I wanted to tell him about the children. They had been driving me crazy, alone with them all day. And the construction going on next door. Non-stop hammering and drilling. They always stopped for the day before he got home from work. I wanted to tell him my dreams. I wanted to tell him so much. But he wanted to rest. He would eat dinner quickly, then withdraw to his study or watch a TV program with the girls snuggling next to him and Adam on his lap. Only to the children did he show tenderness.

He rarely did say, "I love you." When he proposed, all he said was, "We come from similar backgrounds. We were the lucky ones. We got out of Germany. We could build a life together."

I should have known then! I should have known what a jerk he could be!

The phone rang, breaking the silence in the room. It rang and rang. Gerda just sat there, her head in her hands.

"Mom, it's for you!" shouted Esther.

Gerda got up, walked unsteadily to the kitchen counter, and picked up the extension.

"Yes, Saul, she's safe ... She's back home."

Shivaya visualized the house filled with light. She quietly shut the front door behind her as she left. It was dark outside by now. The moon had not yet risen.

27.

Shivaya rubbed a beeswax candle made by monks in a far-off monastery with rose-scented oil from the hills of southern France. She lit the candle and lay back on the soft purple quilt that covered her bed. As her mind grew quiet, visions gradually came into focus. She felt herself soar in the sky like a gull, as she had done many times before. Each time the feeling grew stronger. She could feel the wing bones, the feathers reach out into the ether to hold her aloft. She found she could steer in any direction she wished and that houses and buildings grew clearer in their shapes beneath her. She soared in the direction of the house she had recently left, soared over the roof on which Hannah had hidden. She merged the seagull in the sky with her body on her bed and sent healing waves of energy to Hannah, to Gerda, to Esther and to the toddler, Adam, who must sense the turmoil around him. She sent waves of light to their troubled souls. But it was Hannah who gripped her. So passionate, so dark, so troubled, yet with rays of pure light. It would be her mission to save the girl whose spirit was infused with gold.

She fell asleep. The candled burned down and flickered out. Shivaya soared in her dreams, soared through the sky over the ocean to far-off lands, finally to return to the body, where she awoke at dawn, clear-headed and famished for food.

28.

Gerda looked at herself in the full-length bedroom mirror. Pendulous white breasts. Fat thighs. Stretch marks from her pregnancies. A thick scar from a long-ago appendectomy. Hair like pale straw. The face—sad—like the figurehead of a woman on a ship's prow. The slant of the brows, as though some Mongol tribesman had planted his seed in a Jewish great-grandmother. Pale blue eyes.

I used to be beautiful, with long waist-length hair, and I was skinny. Too skinny even. I'd just been through a rotten relationship, and I guess Saul was still suffering over Nina. "A good man from a good Jewish family," people said. "He has a future." My uncle and aunt urged me to marry you. "An actress you want to be? You'll end up penniless. How will you raise children?" they asked. "Without a good provider."

I wasn't even sure I wanted children.

"Do you love me?" I asked on our wedding night.

"Yes," you said, and you held me close for a long time. Your voice was tender. "With all my heart I love you."

But this had all changed. Vanished.

She fingered her hair. It had strands of grey. Soon she'd have to tint it. Saul's mother, being so Orthodox, always wore a wig. A brown wig. But Tante Ursula never did. Tante Ursula was hunched over in body and soul.

Mama, I wish you were here. My real mother.

Adam was gurgling to himself. He toddled through the door into her bedroom. She flung a robe around herself and picked him up. "You climbed out of your crib, you bad baby."

She rested her face against his soft dark hair. She carried him into the kitchen, set him down on the linoleum, and gave him two tin plates to play with and bang together while she prepared oatmeal and a bottle of warm milk for him.

He was teething, and he chewed at the edge of the tin plate. Fortunately, the red teething lotion she'd put on his gums last night soothed the pain. The girls would be at school all day. She phoned a neighbor, an older woman who sometimes babysat for Adam, and arranged to drop him off at her house.

An hour later she was on her way to the City. Her fingers clenched the steering wheel, and her heart pounded against her chest. She drove onto the Bay Bridge. Water so deep so far below. She could stop the car, climb a railing, and jump to her death. But what if she didn't die and was maimed? That would be worse than dying.

She found a parking space near the alley by the hotel.

A warm spring breeze blew through her hair and rustled papers that littered the pavement. She was wearing high heels. Stockings. Silky dark blue dress with short sleeves and deep décolletage. A white jacket. Rouge carefully applied gave subtle color to her cheeks. Eye shadow. Perfume. "Evening in Paris." Hair sprayed into a cloud around her face.

She climbed the familiar stairs, smelled the familiar odor of something stale and gingery, and knocked at his door. She hadn't seen him since December.

No answer. Just as she was about to leave, the door opened, and a young man with tousled black hair in a terry cloth bathrobe appeared.

"What do you want?"

"The man who used to live here—the German—is he still here?"

The man looked puzzled. "The German? I don't know who you're talking about."

"He used to live here."

"We moved in just last week. Sorry I can't help."

"Hey Jerry, who is it?" called a female voice.

"Someone asking about a man who used to live here."

"Come back to bed."

"Sorry I can't help," he said again with an apologetic smile, and he closed the door.

She sank down on the cold splintery wooden floor, head in her hands, and sobbed.

Moments later, she descended the stairs and knocked at the manager's door. A plump, fair-haired woman answered the knock.

"No," she said in response to Gerda's questions. "I have no idea where he moved. He left back in January."

The weather had grown grey and chilly by the time she stumbled along the pavement towards her car. She sat inside it for a long time, absolutely motionless, before she finally turned the key of the ignition, released the brake, put her foot on the gas, and, still half in a daze, set the car in gear.

At Barbara's house she collapsed in tears.

"It's okay, honey," Barbara said. Her warm voice comforted Gerda. "I love you. Men are jerks!" Gerda flung her arms around Barbara's neck and clung to her, as if she were clinging to a ship's mast in the ocean. The feel of Barbara's warm bosom, the perfumed smell of her flesh comforted her.

She sobbed and sobbed, unable to stop the torrent of tears. She felt as if her last hope had somehow vanished. Then she opened her eyes, wiped them, pulled away, and something in Barbara's expression, perhaps the curve of her lips, a slight curve that suggested contempt, something in the look of Barbara's eyes made Gerda wary. Just as she had always suspected, Barbara was an enemy in disguise. A masked imposter.

Her fingers trembled as she picked up her car keys from the coffee table in Barbara's living room and grabbed her purse from the floor.

29.

Since Saul had begun working late, he usually drove to work at the Lab instead of taking the bus. He came home only to eat a hasty dinner and watch the ten o'clock news before going to sleep. The occasion of this intense work was an upcoming conference in Frankfurt where he would present a paper on halide compounds at a conference of inorganic chemists from all over the world. He was going to return to the land that had cast him out, the land from which he had barely escaped with his life. The prospect filled him with excitement and fear.

As he sipped his instant coffee, he idly surveyed the walls of his laboratory, ignoring the pinups, as he thought about the day's work. His fingers trembled as he lit a fire beneath a burner; his hands trembled as he poured a minute quantity of a solution into a beaker.

His thoughts traveled back to the railroad journey across the border into France. He had huddled with others in the Youth Aliya group in the cold, crowded third class compartment, while one of their leaders conferred in a low voice with officials; money must have changed hands because they were not asked for their papers.

Now he would be returning as a guest. Those affable

Germans whom he would meet, had they grown up in view of the smoke that rose from the camps? What did they secretly feel about Jews, whom they were now welcoming back, with an apparent national outburst of conscience?

He set these thoughts aside as he focused on his experiments. "You are moving into a new level of aware-ness," Shivaya said when he told her about a recent dream he vaguely remembered in which he had been attending a class on chemistry. They were lying in her bed, having just made love. The fragrance of her body filled the air, the sensation of being inside the tight wetness of her sex lingering with him. Sheltered by her. The softness of her breasts. The smoothness of her skin.

He told her of his sense of having been an alchemist in a former life, the sense of familiarity he felt when he first began working with chemical elements. "Yes," she murmured. "I can feel that you were one. I also feel that you were a healer. But that ability has lain dormant until now." She nestled closer. "You could be so much more than you have allowed yourself to be," she murmured in her soft voice.

"Really?" he said. Perhaps his past life memories were wishful fantasies. Her last statement disturbed him. He strode naked into the kitchen and poured himself a glass of water. What was he doing here with this woman who dealt in far-off realms of fantasy.

What could he do? How was he failing to be all that he could be? He worked so hard; he tried so hard to do everything right. Maybe this woman, so tempting, so persuasive with her Scandinavian accent and her clear grey eyes, was a trifle crazy. A spiritual prostitute, as Gerda called her, peddling her wares.

Shivaya shivered with cold and pulled the sheet over her. Saul was closing himself off out of fear. Sadly, she realized he lacked some core of courage. But still, she craved his touch.

"Come back to bed," she murmured.

She reached up and pulled him down towards her, and he let himself be drawn once again into the soft tenderness of her body.

At eight A.M. the alarm rang, rousing him from sleep. He wanted more than anything to keep on sleeping. But it was Saturday. Time for him to drive back to his apartment, shower and shave, swallow coffee, eat a piece of toast, then pick up the children.

"Stay," Shivaya whispered into his ear. "Sweetheart, let yourself rest just for today."

Why not? he thought. For once the children can do without me. I'm always so punctual, but I'm human. Drowsily he sat up, took a deep breath, reached for the phone by the bedside table, and dialed.

30.

June, 1976

Gerda dreamed about Saul. When she woke up, his side of the bed was cold. The luminous clock showed one-fifteen A.M. She felt an irresistible urge to call him. If he was sleeping, he usually left the phone off the hook so that it sounded a busy signal. Trembling, she picked up the receiver from the night table and dialed his number. No answer. She called again and again. Each time no answer.

At six A.M. she called again, and once more at seven. At eight o'clock he called to say in a tight voice that he couldn't take the children this weekend because something had come up.

"You were with that whore all night."

The receiver clicked off.

Damn him! She poured herself another cup of coffee, laced it with whiskey. The children were making so much noise. Those girls, giggling in their room. Saturday morning. Adam wandered into the kitchen. His diaper hung precariously between his thighs. Wet and soaking. Had to change him. Damn Saul! Leaving her with all this while he whored around!

She slammed the coffee cup down on the table so hard that it splattered coffee on her robe and on the table top.

"Adam, come here!"

He toddled in the opposite direction.

She got up, clambered after him, and scooped him into her arms. Ugh! Shitty diaper!

After she had changed and fed him, and after the girls had finished their messy breakfast of cornflakes and orange juice and toast smeared with jam, she got dressed. Old khaki pants and a loose white blouse. Warm summer day. Oh, she wanted to kill that bastard!

She had to get out of the house! Take the girls and Adam with her since Saul had stood them up! She'd drive them all to Tilden Park. Let the girls walk with Adam around Jewel Lake while she sat under a tree and read the paperback novel that she had slipped into her purse.

The children made a din in the back seat as she drove!

"Quiet!" she yelled.

They ignored her.

I will kill them, she thought, crazy with rage as she thought about his words. "Something has come up." Yes, his cock had come up with that horrible Danish woman!

I will kill them. Yes I will kill them, she thought, as she sped down a long, steep, winding slope. I will kill us all. The trees ahead loomed invitingly. Yes, she could crash against a trunk, a solid thick trunk, and all of them would die.

Life was too hard. She wanted to die. She would kill his brats, like Medea in the Greek myth. Tears blinded her as she drove heedlessly around curves. "Mom, be careful!" shouted Hannah.

She pressed harder on the gas pedal.

They were going sixty, seventy . . .

"Mom, stop!" cried Esther.

Wedged between the two girls in the back seat, Adam began howling.

The din of their voices and his cries rang in her ears, creating in her an even greater frenzy. She careened along the road, still going far too fast, and an oak tree loomed up ahead. Why not crash into it and end this nightmare?

Hannah clutched her from behind. "Stop!" she screamed. "Stop!"

In a daze, Gerda pressed down hard on the brake pedal, gears grinding as she stopped. She leaned over the wheel and wept. Esther stared straight ahead, eyes glazed in shock. Adam was crying, while Hannah's soft hands caressed her mother's shoulders.

Later that day, after an early dinner of soup and toast, Gerda retreated to her bedroom, and Hannah, concerned, followed and sat down on the edge of the bed where her mother lay curled on her side.

"You're my best child," Gerda murmured. She straightened her body, sat up, and caressed Hannah's hair, dark and curly like Saul's. "You're the most sensitive. You love me." She leaned over and kissed the top of Hannah's head. Hannah felt strange, as she had once before, as if something of her mother had passed into her and was filling her.

I hate you. I want to strangle you sometimes, Mom. You can be so mean, so crazy, and you can say things that hurt so much.

It was dusk. The light in the room had darkened. She felt both her mother's pain and sorrow and this strange feeling inside herself. Later she wandered into Adam's bedroom. He was still sleeping in a crib, although by now he could easily climb out over the railing. She looked down at the small body, his soft skin, his downy hair. He wore light blue flannel pajamas printed with images of cars and airplanes.

She could choke him in his sleep. Her hands tingled. Why did she feel this way? She loved him, yes, she loved him. She could creep into her mother's room later and choke her. Choke them all to get rid of this horrible feeling inside her.

She left the bedroom, walked out of the house, and slammed the door behind her. It was raining. She was wearing only shorts and a T-shirt, and she was barefoot. She began to run, disregarding how the brambles and concrete hurt her feet.

31.

Hannah wandered along the BART tracks, kicking rusty cans that lay in the dry grass. A voice kept going through her head. She would hear herself talking to her mother, and she could not stop talking. Words running on record grooves. Around and around on the surface.

Skating on a surface of words.

Going around. And around. And around.

She could not get beneath the surface of the words to the reality of her core. So many fears lay in that dark fluid beneath the impenetrable membrane of words that kept spinning around in record rim grooves. If only she could stop them from running around in her mind like frightened mice.

If only there were someone to understand.

A voice kept telling her to do crazy things. To die. Yes, die to escape the pain of these words that ran around in her mind, wearing her out, giving her no peace. You are bad, said the voice. Rotten. You are killing your mother because you are mean and heartless. Why go on living? Why go on consuming air and food and water? Die, said the voice.

A train hooted in the distance. She put her foot on the

closest rail. If the train ran over it, she would become a cripple. Punishment for all the bad thoughts, for wanting to kill her baby brother, for all the crazy, mean thoughts that ran through her mind. She could throw herself underneath the wheels of the train.

Die. Die. Go on. Do it, said the voice.

The thought hovered, like a black bird that grew larger and larger, crowding out all other thoughts. She walked across the track and put her foot on the slender wooden plank that lay above the electric third rail. Death was easily within her reach.

Holding very still, all her muscles tensed, she heard the whistle of an approaching train, saw it grow from a speck in the distance into an ever larger, long dark train winding around curves. Then, as it loomed huge, she drew back in spite of herself, flung herself on the ground, heard its wheels grind against the metal rails, felt its wind around her. Coward, she thought. I am a coward. Tears streamed down her face. She shrieked into the empty air.

Eyes closed, for an instant she saw herself multiplied, as if she were looking at herself through a kaleidoscope. God help me, she prayed. God help me. It was something inside her speaking that was only a part of her. There was no answer. Only that gigantic black bird moving its huge wings through her mind.

32.
October, 1976

Shortly after the plane landed with a jolt, Saul heard the blonde stewardess give instructions for deplaning. She spoke in German. That soft slurry German voice that nevertheless could become so harsh.

He felt as if he were in an ominous dream. Why had he agreed to return to a land where he and his kind were not wanted? Forty-five years ago they would have killed him. *Schmutzig Juden. Dirty Jew. Kike. Scum of the earth.* Now they welcomed him back, summoning him as an honored guest to present his research findings.

He followed the line of passengers to the main terminal. A man in a chauffeur's cap was waving a large white cardboard sign with his name in big black letters.

"Doktor Steinhart?"

"Yes. It's me," said Saul.

"Come this way, *bitte.*"

The chauffeur spoke a few words to an official who ushered Saul swiftly through customs. Outside the airport it was a cold and cloudy September day. The chauffeur led Saul to a black limousine, and as they drove through the city Saul saw how much Frankfurt had changed. The old buildings and narrow streets for the most part had given way to broad, traffic-heavy streets and stark modern buildings. There was still, however, an atmosphere of Germanic cleanliness. Lack of litter on the well-swept streets, manicured public gardens and iron grilled fences.

He wondered if the five-hundred-year-old building in which his family had lived still existed, and if it did, who lived there now? Would there still be geraniums planted in the kitchen window box? Had the building been bombed during the war or razed afterwards to make way for taller, more modern buildings? How strange it felt to return. This was the country in which his family had lived for so many hundreds of years that it seemed it must be embedded in his DNA.

The hotel was among the most luxurious and expensive in the City. Germany valued its scientists. His third-floor room had French doors that opened onto a small balcony. He walked out onto the balcony and looked out over the street below. Across the way was a tiny park with linden trees, grass, and well-trimmed bushes, bordered by a black wrought-iron grilled fence. The leaves were beginning to turn gold and russet. A man dressed in a dark business suit rode by on a bicycle.

He began to unpack his suitcase. In it was underwear, neatly folded shirts—his mother had taught him how to fold in exact thirds—socks, a necktie, grooming implements, an extra pair of shoes, and an extra pair of trousers. He was wearing his tweed jacket and charcoal flannel trousers. It was cold and would get colder. He would need to buy a warm coat.

There was a knock on the door. The bellboy appeared, a skinny lad with a pale, pimply face, dressed in a navy and gilt uniform. Would you like anything from the restaurant downstairs? Food? Beer? No, *danke*. He closed the door on the young boy. In the thirties, would he have belonged to the Hitler Youth who pursued Saul through the streets, knocked him to the ground and kicked him?

However this world was so well-ordered.

Trains and subways and buses ran on time.

The streets were bare of litter.

Everything was clean, orderly, and efficient.

Hotel staff members were impeccably polite.

But he felt danger in the air and all around him. Beneath the façades of civility lay something savage yet meticulously cruel. "Germany is going through a postwar crisis of national guilt," a Jewish colleague had remarked. "But underneath, nothing has changed."

He decided to venture forth onto the street and look for a tobacco shop. As he entered the hotel lobby with its soft lighting, oak paneling, and maroon carpet, he encountered two colleagues whom he knew from former conferences. They were already flushed with drink.

"Come and join us in the bar, *amico,*" said the first, who came from Rome. Short and plump, he spoke English with a slight accent.

"Maybe later," said Saul.

"Come on, mate," said the second, a tall, fair-haired Australian, flinging his arm around Saul's shoulders.

"Thank you, but I have an errand to do. Maybe later."

"We will expect you," said the Italian. *"Achtung!"* He broke into a crazy grin, saluted, and clicked his heels in mock Nazi salute.

Achtung! A shiver ran through Saul. He remembered an SS officer demanding that a Jewish peddler salute him, and when the peddler hesitated for an instant, the officer knocked the old man to the pavement and stamped on his withered arthritic fingers, shouting in rage.

Saul excused himself, returned to his room, and lay down. He could feel a migraine coming on. He went into the spacious bathroom with its marble fixtures, dampened a washcloth with cold water, lay down, and pressed it over his forehead. But despite all his efforts at envisioning light around him, dark shadows of the past kept closing in.

33.

Shivaya was dreaming that she held a weeping Hannah in her arms when a knock awakened her. Drowsy with sleep, she rubbed her eyes, sat up in bed, pulled away the quilt, and shivered with cold. In the dark she felt with her toes until she found her suede slippers and wedged her feet into them.

"Let me in," a voice whispered. More knocking. "Please." It was a young girl's voice.

As if it were a continuation of the dream, Shivaya opened the door. Dark wavy hair flowed over a hunched little back. Slender fingers with bitten-off nails. Shivaya put her arms around the girl, pressing her against the soft silk of her nightgown. "Come in." Hannah stumbled inside. For a long time Shivaya just held her.

"I want to stay with you," Hannah sobbed. "It's too rough at home. Mom is always screaming at me or at my brother or sister. Mostly at me."

"How did you find me?"

"You gave me your card long ago. I kept it."

Shivaya led her to the couch, where Hannah curled up against the cushions. She rubbed a swollen purplish spot beneath the girl's right eye. " Did she hit you?"

"Yes."

"Does your father know?"

"He's off in Germany."

"I know," said Shivaya. Anger surged up in her. Why couldn't Saul protect this girl? Why couldn't he stand up to Gerda?

"Are you sleeping with my Dad?" Hannah asked, her voice tremulous.

"Yes," murmured Shivaya.

"Mom said you were. But I could tell, anyway. It doesn't matter to me," she said in a flat voice. "I just don't know where to go."

"Rest awhile," said Shivaya. "I'll make you a cup of chamomile tea."

Where could Hannah go and be safe? As she waited for the water to boil, Shivaya thought of a Buddhist retreat in the Santa Cruz mountains she'd visited in the past. A few eccentric hippies lived there, peaceful and tolerant, so she thought.

The phone rang. Shivaya let it ring until it finally stopped. She could feel Gerda's energy in the sound.

"I bet it's my Mom," said Hannah. "She must have found out I'm gone."

"Yes," said Shivaya. "She goes wild with that phone."

When it rang again, Shivaya took the phone off the hook. By now the tea was ready. She brought it into the living room and settled next to Hannah on the sofa.

"I don't want to go back," said Hannah.

"How would you like to go on a trip?"

Hannah took a sip of the tea, then asked, "Where?"

"A place where you can rest and heal."

"Mom will have a fit if I run away. She'll have the

police out looking for me."

"I'll deal with her."

"Where can I go?"

"Somewhere beautiful in the mountains. I know a place I think you'll like."

"Well … okay," said Hannah, still in the flat voice. She set down the cup on the coffee table, wiping the wet bottom so it would not leave a mark on the glass-covered surface. What could be worse than her present situation? She thought of that day at the railroad tracks. It didn't matter too much if she lived or died.

"We'll have fun. It will all work out. You'll see," said Shivaya.

The candle she had lit gave both their faces a soft glow.

"Now lie down here on the sofa and try to sleep for a few hours because we're going to leave very early in the morning."

She got a couple of blankets and a pillow from the hall closet and put them on the sofa for Hannah. Then she herself went back to bed. She needed to be rested for the journey ahead. What she was preparing to do could cost her dearly, although she *had* to do it. If Hannah remained at home, the poison from her mother would seep inwards, transforming into self-hatred.

At four A.M. Shivaya got up and brewed strong coffee which Hannah sipped. She nibbled at a slice of toast. Shivaya put on a pair of jeans, a heavy sweater, her hiking shoes, and found an extra ski jacket for Hannah. She scribbled a note temporarily canceling her classes and posted it outside the door.

"Are you sure this is going to be okay? I'm scared."

"It will be more than okay," said Shivaya with a

confidence that she did not feel.

They descended the apartment stairs quietly, so as not to wake the neighbors, went into the garage, and got into Shivaya's van. It was still dark outside when they hit the freeway. Then the sky began to lighten with dawn. By the time they reached San Jose, the sun had just risen over the edge of the horizon.

Hannah was crying silently as they drove. Shivaya patted her shoulder in sympathy. They turned off the freeway onto a steep, winding road. It was slippery with recent rain. The van skidded. Shivaya braked, just missing a ditch.

At the summit of the mountains was a restaurant where they stopped for a breakfast of scrambled eggs, toast, and coffee. Shivaya stepped outside and made a call from the public phone booth.

Then they kept on going until they reached the Santa Cruz beach. The sky was grey with morning fog, and the sea, too, was grey, with white-capped waves breaking against the shore. Shivaya parked, and they got out of the van, took off their shoes, rolled up their pants, and waded in, laughing as the icy water submerged their feet and ankles. Hannah shrieked happily, even as a wave soaked the bottom of her jeans.

"Come on, we've got to get warm and get you some dry pants," said Shivaya.

They walked along a narrow street crowded with shops and went into one which displayed a large peace sign above its door. While Hannah browsed through the aisles, Shivaya found armfuls of brightly colored sweaters, several pairs of pants, two scarves, two ski caps, and some faded but clean underwear "Try these on," she said to Hannah.

"I don't want you to catch pneumonia." She pointed to the makeshift dressing room with its curtain.

"All these?"

"You'll need clothing."

They ate fish and chips at a beach side café. Famished from the ocean air and the cold, Hannah greedily devoured hers. Afterwards they walked along the beach again. By now the sun had burned away the fog, and the sea sparkled as white-capped waves broke against the shore. The cold wind whipped sand against their faces as the ocean waves sounded in a dull rhythm.

"I love it here," said Hannah. "I want to stay here forever."

"I wish we could," said Shivaya. "But it's not safe. The police will be looking for you. I've got to get back and teach my classes. We're going to a place in the mountains. It's secluded, and they won't look there. I think you'll like it."

"Really?" Hannah sounded doubtful.

"Really."

Hannah stooped to pick up a greyish green stone.

"Look," she said. "Could this be jade?"

Shivaya took the stone from Hannah and felt its vibrations. "Perhaps," she said. "This stretch of shore used to be littered with semi-precious stones. People have taken most of them. It's good to have a special stone. It gives you strength."

It was early afternoon when they began the drive back up the mountain along Highway 17. The road was shaded beneath steep, forested slopes. There were lingering patches of snow.

As they drove, Hannah was silent. Shivaya tried to send her calming energy and to calm her own fears. What in

God's name was she doing? This could land her in jail for kidnapping. She could be deported. But Hannah needed this escape now. Later it would be too late.

She turned off the highway and descended a steep winding dirt road. Shivaya hoped it was the right one. It had been a long time since her last visit. She breathed with relief when they approached a cluster of steep-roofed wooden buildings. A battered pickup, a VW camper, and a dusty sedan were parked in front.

She parked next to the sedan. They got out of the van and walked along a flagstone path, up a flight of steps to a porch with a bench and a ragged stuffed armchair. A heavy metal bell hung from a rope. When Shivaya rang it, no one answered. Finally she opened the door, and they entered a sunny, spacious kitchen. Pots and pans hung along the walls. A large chopping table stood in the center of the room. Two stainless steel sinks and a stainless steel counter filled the far corner. A delicious smell of baking bread wafted from the oven.

"Anyone here?" Shivaya called out.

A gaunt woman with long white hair, dressed in jeans and a red sweater, emerged. "Shivaya!" she cried, and she gave Shivaya a big hug. "It's good to see you again!"

She led them into a warm living room that smelled of smoke. A fire burned in the stove. It glowed orange behind the glass. The high ceiling sloped, and it had rough beams.

"I need to speak with Marge for a while," said Shivaya. "Hannah, relax and make yourself at home."

Hannah stretched out on a braided rug in front of the blazing stove. How cozy it felt. For a while she dozed off. Then she stood up and looked around her. She was alone in the living room, which held several comfortable chairs and couches. She began to browse through the bookshelves that lined the walls. There were books on Buddhism, on mystical subjects, on psychology, a few novels, and a worn copy of a Latin grammar. Near the door hung a silver-framed photo of an Asian monk in a black robe. Several lines in Japanese were written beneath it on ivory parchment paper.

Shivaya and Marge returned. "You can stay with us if you like," said Marge. "I understand your situation."

Hannah's face expressed doubt.

"Try it for a few days."

Just then a man of about thirty-five, with a growth of beard and a ruddy weather-beaten face, wearing an aged leather jacket, jeans, and heavy boots, walked into the room.

"We have a guest. She may be with us for a while," said Marge. "Ted, this is Hannah."

His eyes shone, and he gave off a warm glow. "Good to have you here." He put his arm around her shoulder. She flinched.

"Don't scare her," said Marge. "Come, Hannah, I'll show you the women's dorm."

They walked along a dirt path to a low-slung wood-framed building and entered a room with a futon on the bare floor, hand-sewn muslin curtains, and an electric heater in the corner.

"I'll bring you some bedding," said Marge.

Shivaya hugged Hannah goodbye.

Afterwards, when she was alone, Hannah ran her hands over the rough plank walls, felt the draft that came through the thin pane windows, and shivered. She clutched the gemstone from the beach in her pocket, but it gave cold comfort.

34.

Now she'd done it! Visions of police, handcuffs, sirens, and flashing lights ran through her mind as she drove back down the mountain. They could put her in jail and send her back to Denmark with no hope of return. But she'd *had* to do it. She'd seized the instant of time where hope was possible!

She prayed to the Goddess for protection. Her hands trembled as she drove, and the van swerved towards the center of the road. Just then a deer made its way softly towards her from the left and stood absolutely motionless, almost fading into the foliage. She managed to brake and gazed into its eyes. For a long moment the deer and the woman gazed at each other. The deer did not seem to fear Shivaya.

I am protected, she thought.

It was noon before she reached Santa Cruz. She had time to linger before she drove back for her evening class. The sun had burned through the fog by the time she arrived at the beach. She peeled off her jacket, left it in the van, walked, and watched waves as they broke until her head began to clear of all the thoughts that had been swirling around inside.

Feeling her feet on the earth always grounded her. As she walked, she focused on energy from the earth that rose up through her body. The sound of the waves penetrated her, and the ocean gleamed silver and turquoise beneath the warm midday sun. In the distance she saw a man in a dark windbreaker and faded jeans walking towards her. As he came closer, he looked familiar. She had caught a glimpse of this man months ago in a fish and chips café near Santa Cruz. His face was deeply tanned, his features sharply drawn. When he had come within a few feet of her, he stopped. His gaze met hers. There was a sense of *knowing* him. "I've seen you before," he said. His voice was sharp, New York tinged.

"Yes," she said. "The fish and chips place . . . that was over a month ago."

"Yes, that must be it," he said. His face crinkled when he smiled, and the look in his eyes caused her heart to beat a little faster.

Oh, Shivaya, she told herself. *Don't spin fairy tales out of whole cloth.*

"Would you like a cup of coffee?"

"Yes. I'd love one," she said.

She followed him into a small, crowded café. The room smelled of fried fish. The people seemed to be locals: men and women with long hair, scruffy beach clothing, and weather-beaten faces. He ordered black coffee for both of them. They squeezed into a booth by the window where they could see the boardwalk, empty now that summer tourists had left.

He reached across the narrow table and caressed her cheek. "You have good bones," he said.

"Thank you," she said. "From my father's side, I guess.

I'm Danish."

"You, too! My grandparents came from Denmark!" He talked a little about his life. He had grown up in Brooklyn, studied at the Art Students League, and had a studio for many years in the East Village. After a life-altering trip to India, he had moved to California

"I've always wanted to go to India.."

"You must go! You absolutely *must!*" he said.

He had visited Shivaya's Buddhist retreat, and he knew of others in the Santa Cruz mountains. He listened intently and with apparent understanding as she told him about the workshops that she taught. She looked at her watch. "I've got to be getting back," she said. She sighed and fingered the ashtray on the table. She wanted to stay here with him, wanted this conversation not to end.

"Will I see you again, Shivaya?"

"Yes, I come down on occasion."

"Call me next time you're here." He took a pencil out of his jacket pocket and wrote down his phone number on a napkin with an air of assurance that rankled her.

She gave him one of her business cards. It showed a photo of her in tights and a tank top, her arms and torso arched towards the sky. As he examined her picture, an image of Saul flashed in her mind, and she felt a tinge of guilt. He leaned closer, lowered his voice, and said in a confidential tone, "Shivaya, what's your real name?"

"Katrina," she murmured. It just slipped out of her, without forethought. Immediately she regretted it. She should not have let herself be caught like that! Better to keep that shield of "Shivaya."

"Aha!" His eyes narrowed. He looked up at her again, and their eyes met. They were grey like hers. His face revealed thin lines of age. She took one of his hands between her own and held it for a moment. His hand felt warm and thick. His fingers were strong, the palms calloused. The lines were few, deep and clear-cut. Those of a man who slept deeply, untroubled with insomnia. His nails were blunt, square-cut, with a residue of clay beneath the edges.

"Katrina, call me!" His voice now sounded lower, even urgent. He leaned across the table and kissed her lightly on the lips. In a daze, she watched him pay the cashier. She walked back alone to her van, electric with Jakob's energy. The dull sound of waves broke in her ears; foam glistened on the sand beneath her feet.

35.

He was one of the last speakers. He left the podium to the sound of loud applause from his colleagues, and he felt exuberant. Even had there been no applause, he knew he had done a good job explaining his latest results. He planned to stay on afterwards in Frankfurt to work with a fellow chemist with whom he had exchanged papers over the years.

Some days later he found himself inside the German's lab as they watched halide atoms split under an inflow of mercury. The fragments formed translucent jewel-like waves. Sapphire electrons attached themselves to orange-hued protons, forming entirely new compounds. It was hypnotic to watch the process continually unfold. This state-of-the-art machine functioned both as a high-powered microscope and as a slow motion camera. As always, the Germans were ahead of the game. Even after two world war defeats.

"Amazing," said Saul. He turned to Franz, his German colleague. "It is because of your meticulous work I requested you," Franz had said the first time they met in person over coffee just before the conference. "Many of the other researchers I do not trust. Their results contain questionable elements. But you have always thoroughly documented your work."

The acknowledgment had made Saul glow with pride. However, he still felt a current of unease. Franz was tall, fair-haired, and athletic in build. He wore rimless spectacles and had a kindly expression. In the lab he wore an open-necked shirt, dark trousers, and Birkenstocks with light grey socks. A casual dresser, like Saul himself.

But Saul was sure that Franz would have expressed quite different opinions about his work if this were 1938! Was Franz' father in Hitler's army? Saul did not want to dwell on this thought. Their work together existed in a capsule in which the past did not exist. Yet it still cast its spell powerfully over Saul.

Franz brought homemade sandwiches each day for their lunch. Substantial fare of ham or sausage with cheese on thick rolls or homemade rye bread, which the two men would down with strong black coffee. Saul ate the meat with relish, and a bit of guilt.

Beneath Franz' kindly actions, beneath the affable smiles and polite words of the other German scientists and the hotel staff, what did they really think of him? What if he were to tell Franz about his mother's kosher kitchen? What if he were to tell him of all the hardships and persecutions that he and his family had suffered in Germany?

Later that day Saul leafed through a pile of papers to fill out for the Laboratory back in California. They had given him a small office here with typewriter, copier, and desk. On top of all the papers was a pink message slip from Gerda. He pushed the paper aside. He did not want to call her! Certainly it could wait.

At six o'clock in the evening Franz closed the office, bid Saul farewell and went home. He was looking forward to a weekend in his country house with the wife and three tow-haired children whose photos graced his office.

The weekend stretched ahead of Saul. In the morning he would sleep late. Instead of going back to his hotel, Saul wandered along the streets. Gerda's pink message slip lay uneasily in his mind, but again he pushed it aside. Could he find his family's old apartment building? How much the city had changed, with its gleaming modern buildings and plazas. There were no traces left of rubble from the wartime bombing, yet entire neighborhoods had been obliterated. The population was far more diverse, with dark-skinned people from Middle Eastern countries. Turks. Greeks. Italians. Yet despite the changes, the city still retained its Germanic order and cleanliness. He walked and walked until it was quite dark, and the streetlight glowed, but he could not find the street where he'd lived as a child. Still he walked on. Eventually he found himself in a dubious neighborhood with neon-lit strip clubs and run-down buildings. A shadowy figure emerged in the darkness, and Saul felt the old childhood fear, as if *"Juden"* blazed in yellow letters from his forehead.

Beyond the brilliant streetlights he could glimpse a far-off crescent moon. He entered a tavern where mingled odors of sausage, beer and cigarette smoke assailed him. The place was crowded and noisy. Heavily made-up women in tight skirts. Arrogant-looking men with shaved heads and heavy chain jewelry gave him pause. There were also sad-looking people hunched over their drinks. If he had not been so hungry, he would have immediately left, but something else also impelled him to stay, as if here he might glimpse the true Germany beneath its façade of civility. He ordered veal cutlets, fried potatoes, and a glass of dark draft beer.

The hostess approached. "Would you share your table?"

"Yes, of course."

A young woman, perhaps in her mid-twenties, sat down opposite him. She was small-boned, with sharp features, tinted blonde hair, bright red nail polish and lipstick. The refinement of her bearing set her apart from the rest.

He had a fleeting vision of a woman whom he had seen at times in frightening dreams. She was German, always blonde, often dressed as a nurse in a white uniform. She would conduct him to showers of gas, where no Jew awakened. This blonde woman also wore white, a low-cut dress of white silk that revealed her full breasts when she leaned forward, as she did, apparently by accident, to glance at the menu. She asked if he were a tourist. Her voice was cultured. She spoke in High Deutsch, not in keeping with the tone of the crowd.

"I'm from California," he said.

"Oh!" her eyes widened. "I'd love to go there."

Somehow, after another glass or two of beer—beers were on the house—perhaps the bartender had slipped in something stronger, he thought afterwards—she no longer appeared as frightening. She twisted a tendril of her hair, which now looked flaxen, and she seemed younger now, even frail, innocent, in need of protection. The painted lips quivered. The blue eyes held a hint of sadness. She was studying anthropology, she said, at the University, and she worked as a model to pay her tuition. They walked out of the restaurant together. It was a balmy night, unseasonably warm for October. She wore a thick lacy shawl over her white dress. It began to rain. They took shelter in a doorway. She shivered.

"My apartment is close," she said. "Why don't you come in until the rain stops."

Her apartment was cluttered with furniture of mixed vintage. An upright piano. A small antique desk littered with student papers. A pothus plant had sprouted long green branches that ran along the molding beneath the ceiling. Whatever the bartender had put into his drink was having an effect.

"Do you have any coffee?"

"But yes, of course."

She went into the kitchen while he dozed on the sofa, and a few minutes later she came back with small, elegant cups of espresso. *"Trinken."* The coffee was strong and bitter, with a chicory taste.

She took off her high heels and put her feet on his lap. He caressed her toes through the filmy nylon stockings.

"You're cold," he said.

"You can warm me up."

The softness of her body, with all its curves. Her breasts. Her thighs. The fuzz of dark blonde pubic hair. She had put a red silk scarf over the bedside lamp which cast a reddish glow over everything.

Making love with the enemy.

The golden forbidden girls of his childhood.

He thought of the pretty girl with long blonde braids who lived on the floor beneath theirs in Frankfurt. He had been forbidden to play with her. When they were older, he had seen her outside on the steps, giggling with her boyfriend.

Shikse. Verboten. Forbidden.

Turning his back, he undressed, and rolled on top of her. She was moist and eager. She clutched his buttocks, and he thrust hard and deep. She moaned with pleasure, and then lay back, sated. They lay quietly for a few moments. She lit a cigarette and offered him one. He refused. Then she sat up, pulled back the quilt, and gazed at his body. She put down the cigarette, took his penis between her fingers and felt its tip.

"Circumcised," she murmured.

He flinched and pulled away.

"You are Jewish?"

"Yes."

She bit her lips, as if she were about to speak and thought better of it.

He quickly put on his clothes and left.

Afterwards he walked and walked along the streets, exhausted but compelled to continue. Although he walked until the early hours of the morning, he could not find the building where he used to live. After a few hours of restless sleep in his hotel room, he woke up and went out to his balcony. It was much colder. The sky had filled with pale wintry clouds.

36.

Hannah had been gone now for three days.

Three days of hell.

The police had found no clues.

Gerda paced back and forth across the house, flung herself down on the bed, picked up the phone, and put it down several times.

Saul, why can't you be here for me when I need you? Bastard! Off at a conference. Probably fucking a German waitress. No, you're too uptight for that. If only you hadn't left, none of this would have happened. You abandoned me and the children. All my fault ...

Unable to bear it any longer, she phoned the Lab. They refused to give out any information as to his whereabouts. Maybe Shivaya knew. Maybe he had called her. That whore!

She, Gerda, was no longer a human being to him.

He had no pity for her.

He had no love for her.

How then could he have ever loved her, because love does not die?

Their marriage had been built on a false foundation.

She was walking on the edge of a moon glacier.

She was not human to him. So how could she be human to herself?

Oh Hannah, my treasure, you are the one who makes me human. Why have I been so cruel to you?

Naked, a blue towel around her shampooed wet hair, she went into the kitchen and poured herself a shot of scotch at ten o'clock in the morning.

Thank God Esther was at school and the car pool driver had picked up Adam for the nursery school he had recently begun attending.

Thank God she could be who she was for a few hours. Stop being a mother and wearing clothes and wiping Adam's runny nose and all the rest that sucked energy out of her until she was empty of herself.

Goddamn Shivaya! She was sure that Saul had called her from Germany.

Picking up the phone, this time she overcame her hesitation and dialed Shivaya's number. "I need to speak with you," she said. "Can I come over?" Her voice was loud and grating. Shivaya held the receiver a few inches away from her ear.

"Yes," she said reluctantly, in her softest Danish accent.

When Gerda entered Shivaya's apartment, the energy shifted. Shivaya grounded herself with all her strength so as not to be swept away. She visualized light filling the room, light to dissolve the dark flames of Gerda's aura.

"Where is Hannah?"

"I have no idea," said Shivaya.

"You should know. You're psychic!"

"Truly, I don't."

"Did you know she was gone?"

"No," Shivaya lied.

Gerda described how Hannah had disappeared three days ago. "Help me find her!"

Shivaya drew up earth energy through her body. She had to protect Hannah at all costs. She stood absolutely still, withstanding the force of Gerda's energy. "I see her surrounded with light," she said. "We can both do this. It will protect her."

"Bullshit!" Gerda stamped her feet in rage. She was wearing sandals that showed her bony toes, one of which was a little crooked, with peeling red polish. "I don't believe that shit!"

"Then why are you here?"

"Because . . . Did Saul call you?"

"No, I haven't heard from him," Shivaya said truthfully. In her dream last night he had come to her weeping. He had a tender heart, difficult to perceive at first because of all the fences he had built around himself. But last night, in her dream, she wanted to hold him and comfort him. He had a heart as delicate as a flower. A heart too easily crushed, yet made brittle from grief.

"I think you do know where she is." A crafty look came over Gerda's face. Her eyes seemed to slant as in medieval paintings, thought Shivaya, in which everyone seemed touched by a shadow of evil.

"I don't know," said Shivaya. (And who knows, perhaps Hannah had fled the Buddhist center.) "I will send her lots of light. A protective cocoon of light. That is what you can do, too."

"No!" Gerda collapsed on the sofa in tears, and she beat her head against the cushions.

Shivaya sat down beside her, laid her warm hands on Gerda's head, stroked her hair, then massaged her neck and shoulders with a firm touch. Gerda did not resist, but lay there and slowly grew more quiet.

Then she heaved with sobs. "How can I forgive myself?" she moaned. "I drove her away."

"There . . . There . . . it's all right," crooned Shivaya. "Put her in the hands of God. Surround her with light."

"Bullshit!" shrieked Gerda. "There is no God! There is no light. There are no auras. You're a fake, Shivaya! A whore!" She stormed out of the apartment, slamming the door so hard behind her that everything rattled.

Shivaya sat quietly, stunned for a few moments. Then she got up and sprinkled the room with purified water into which she had dropped a few crystals of sea salt. She lit three white candles and sat motionless as she gazed at the flame that flickered above the tallest candle.

After a while she heard rumbling, whether from inside her head or from outside, she did not know. A sudden breeze rustled through the curtains, although the windows were shut. There was a faint scent of roses. Her body felt light, and electricity pulsed through her. The Wiccan goddess had descended to protect her.

37.

When Hannah woke up in the morning, at first she did not know where she was. Her head spun. The room with its bare white walls and plank floor was unfamiliar. Then she remembered that she was in the mountains, far away from home. It was calm here. The air was fresh and smelled of pine and laurel. She could hear birds chirp amidst the trees. In the morning she would wake up to the cries of roosters, because they raised hens and roosters. Each morning at five forty-five, while it was still dark, a bell began to ring in loud tones. She would rouse herself from the warmth of the down sleeping bag, pull on a heavy sweater, warm socks, and hiking boots from the free box, and still in her pajamas, she would trudge to the *zendo*, a large wood-framed building surrounded by trees. She would enter the meditation room, where a log fire glowed in the central fireplace, and she would join the others who were already seated on their black meditation cushions.

"Don't judge your thoughts," Ted remarked as they walked back to the kitchen one day. By now, at seven o'clock in the morning, the sky was light. "Don't push them down or cling to them." But that was almost impossible. Thoughts whirled crazily through her mind.

Still, the meditation helped calm her, she thought. And now she had to focus on the eggs that she was stirring in the pan for their breakfast while Brigitte, a brown-robed nun from Germany, sliced homemade bread. Brigitte's head was shaved, and she wore no makeup. She was, perhaps in her early twenties, just a few years older than Hannah, and she was beautiful. Hannah wondered what had caused Brigitte to choose this life.

Hannah was hungry. The eggs and toast with orange marmalade tasted wonderful. She sipped her coffee, strong and bitter, enjoyed the warmth of the china mug against her cold fingers, and surveyed the group around her. All the residents were here for breakfast, seated around the varnished oak table in the dining area. There was Marge, who nearly always wore the same red sweater, and there was Ted, tall and bearded, whose blue eyes shone with warmth. Joe, a man in his sixties, walked with the aid of a cane. He had been a pilot in the Second World War. There was Sergio, thin and intense, who always wore black and who scowled at Hannah if she entered the *zendo* late. Then there was Molly, cheerful and overweight, with flaming red hair, who only came to the evening meditation. This morning a stranger was with them, a shaggy, bearded man in ragged clothing who said he was just passing through. Hannah wondered what lay in their pasts. What had brought them here to a mountain forest, so far from the rest of the world.

A silver-framed photo of a monk in black robes hung on the wall of the living room. Black ink calligraphy in Japanese was written beneath on white parchment. Marge had told her that this monk's name was Hakuin, that he had been raised in Japan, and that he had founded this community nearly a decade ago. He was a truly enlightened being, she said. A wild, saintly monk. He wanted this place to be a refuge, not only for Buddhists, but for anyone who had spiritual aspirations. "I wish he came here more often," said Marge. She moved closer to Hannah and put her arm around the girl's shoulder. Morning sun shone brightly through the windows and gleamed on the oak dining table. "We never know when he'll show up . . . Come now. It's time to get started on the laundry."

Every day there were chores. Sometimes Hannah helped Marge sew curtains on the old-fashioned Singer or lugged dirty sheets and towels into the washing machine that stood in the barn. They hung the clean laundry on a rope strung between trees to dry. Brigitte, wearing jeans and a sweatshirt, showed Hannah how to clean the men's and women's bathrooms. Her favorite work was helping Ted outside. She learned how to hammer sheetrock for a new cabin they were building; she hauled logs for firewood. He was fun to work with. His jocular spirits helped lighten the seriousness of the Buddhist atmosphere.

"I'm a fuckup," he said cheerfully one starry, cold night when he and Hannah took a walk up through the woods.

"How so?"

"I forged someone's signature on a bank account. I was in jail for three years. I'm still on probation. My family has written me off. My father was a Harvard man, and I'm a disgrace to the family."

"Why did you do it?'

"I wanted to see if I could get away with it. I was young and foolish. I was working at the time for an investment firm on Wall Street. They were more clever than I gave them credit for, or else I was just more stupid, a fuckup. So I've decided to do no more harm. At least here I'm harmless."

"You give a lot to the people here," she said. "You work hard."

"I enjoy it. I want to give back. I like these people. They're laid back. They don't lay their trips on you."

"Do you think you'll stay?"

"Who knows? Some day I may hit the road and disappear."

Dry leaves and twigs creaked beneath their shoes. Hannah saw a blurry animal swiftly cross their path and heard the light sound of its hoofs. The deer, she knew, came out at night. She felt like a deer, shy and beautiful and fragile. They walked on in silence. She felt safe with him. He was like a big brother, one she'd never had and always wanted.

"Who else comes here?" she asked.

"Wayfarers," he said. "Wanderers on the path of karma. We also have patrons who keep us afloat."

Molly invited Hannah to her cabin one afternoon for tea. As water boiled in a kettle on the hot plate, she showed the girl a few pages of the memoir she was writing. The room itself was a mess, with clothing strewn over the floor, the bed, and the unplugged heater. Some of the onionskin pages were yellowed and brittle with age. She settled her ample body onto a folded futon that served as a seat and rubbed her arthritic left knee. "When I was young, I was so thin, you would not have recognized me. I've traveled all over the world. I've lived in India and for a long time in Berkeley. I've had enough men in my life. Much easier to be alone, my dear."

It was when Hannah left Molly's cabin that she saw him. A man with a dark complexion wearing jeans and a white shirt rolled up at the sleeves, open at the neck to reveal a hairless chest, despite the autumn chill in the air. He stood on top of a grassy knoll, and he was chopping a log with a heavy axe. Although his body looked frail, he chopped with muscular vigor. It was Hakuin!

At the evening sitting Hannah saw him once again. This time he wore formal black monk's robes. He sat in full lotus position, legs tucked beneath him. The smoke from the fire made her cough. He looked in her direction. She caught a glimmer of a smile on his lips.

At the end of the sitting, when they had made their bows and chanted the closing chants—words in Japanese with a hypnotic rhythm, but which to Hannah were mere sounds—he addressed the small group, calling the others by name, and then he asked hers. "Hannah," she whispered. "A nice name," he said in a barely audible voice.

He talked about personality as something evanescent. We are not solid, he said. Even our cells consist of particles which can shift into waves of energy. Only our habits form grooves to which we cling. Hannah pondered his words. Afterwards Hakuin walked beside her on the path back to the dining room, where they would gather for evening tea.

"I don't understand about particles," she said.

"You are not a solid being," he said, as dry leaves crunched beneath their feet. "You only think you are. You have the idea that you're solid, but you are really composed of energy, ever shifting energy. Your habits of thought and the ideas that you've taken in give the illusion that you're solid."

"I don't understand."

"Think about it. We know that cells are composed of neutrons, protons, and nuclei, and physicists have discovered even smaller elements. Cells consist of particles that can change into waves of energy that dissolve into the ether. Neither our bodies nor our thoughts are actually solid."

He stopped, took her hands in his, and looked into her eyes. "Who are you, really, Hannah?" His eyes were very dark, and a current of energy ran from his hands through her body. Later that night in bed she felt filled with his energy, and it was difficult to fall asleep.

She dreamed about her mother, and she woke up disturbed. Her stay at Enkoji had been like a balm, a reprieve from life. But her mother's voice began to haunt her. Over the coming days, Hannah felt an increasing need to call her. Ted drove her to a nearby town where there was a public phone booth, so that the call could not be traced. As they drove, she felt as if steel claws were squeezing her mind and her body. With trembling fingers, while Ted shopped for groceries at Safeway, she dialed her home phone number.

"Mom, it's me."

Her mother burst into sobs, then gave a loud cry. "Where are you?"

"In the mountains."

"Hannah, come home!"

"I'm happy here."

"You're breaking my heart!"

Hannah swallowed. "Mom, I love you."

The voice, angry and venomous. "No use hiding, Hannah. The police will find you. They'll put you in a foster home. You're selfish. You think of no one but yourself!"

Hannah hung up. Her eyes stung with tears. The black plastic receiver felt sweaty in her hand as she placed it back in its cradle. "We are not solid. The self is an illusion, ever shifting." Hakuin's words flitted through her mind, but she felt all too heavy, as if she could sink onto the pavement inside the narrow booth.

She wept all the way back as she rode in Ted's dusty Volvo, filled with old newspapers and worn paperbacks. He offered her a Kleenex, which she mutely accepted. Ted, Marge, and the others were kind. But they could not alleviate the venom that filled her. They were like shadows, lacking reality. She sought out Hakuin in vain. He had left the commune for whereabouts unknown, as quietly and mysteriously as he had arrived.

For hours in her sleeping bag that night, she tossed restlessly against its narrow confines. She struggled out of the bag, smashed an empty water glass against the wall, and watched it shatter on the floor. She wanted to smash the kerosene lantern, too, but held back. Instead she grabbed an armful of her clothing, set fire to it in the middle of the room, then hastily blew out the flames. A grey sweater from the free box had become charred at the edges.

38.

In the morning when she walked outside onto the deck, sunlight hit her eyes. She had overslept, and the sun had already risen high in the sky above the trees. *Have to get a broom to sweep up the shards. Hope there's no burn mark on the floor.* As she stumbled down the steps, she nearly ran against the body of a young man bearing a huge backpack. A black guitar case was slung behind the pack and across his shoulders. He was just a little taller than her, and skinny. His face showed a day's growth of beard; his brows were thick and bushy.

"Hey," he said.

"Oh, sorry," she mumbled.

"You look like you're half asleep."

"I am." She was still in her pajamas and a man's oversized sweater.

"No worries. Hey, where's the men's dorm?"

"It's over there." She pointed to a nearby door that also opened onto the deck.

"Hey, you *are* sleepy," he repeated. His voice was soft, even tender. She noticed he had a diamond earring in one ear. His hair was jet black and hung past his shoulders. His eyes shone.

"I'm Sean," he said. "What's your name?"

"Hannah," she mumbled.

"Hey, Hannah, wake up. It's a beautiful day!"

In spite of herself, she smiled.

Later that day, after she had finished her chores, she walked along the trail that led up to the steep hill behind the commune. Behind her she heard footsteps. When she turned around, she saw him there.

"Hannah, is it okay if I join you?" His voice crackled on the edge, a young man's nervousness.

"Yes, it's okay," she said.

They walked in silence side by side as the trail widened.

"This is my favorite spot," she said when they reached the crest. She sat down in the dry grass next to a thick gnarled oak tree, and he sat beside her, a little too close for comfort. They looked out at the hills below, which stretched out into forests of dark trees that merged into the glistening sea and pale sky.

"What brought you here?" she asked.

"I was a sophomore at San Jose State, and I needed some time out." He stared at the horizon, silent for a moment. In profile, his face was pale and rough with acne scars.

"What about you, Hannah?"

She burst into tears. The knife-edge of her mother's voice cut all the way through.

"I'm a bad person," she sobbed. "I'm a bad person. I deserve to die."

"Hannah!"

He put an arm around her and stroked her hair. "You're too young to be thoroughly bad. Don't cry."

But she couldn't stop.

"Tell me what's troubling you," he said.

"I can't."

She kept sobbing, but gradually his hands on her hair and her neck and shoulders soothed her. To feel his body close against her felt so good. His soft jacket smelled of leather mixed with sweat.

At dinner time, she felt self-conscious, and she deliberately sat at the other end of the table from where he was. She talked with Marge, Ted, and Joe, while Sean took his vegetarian beans, brown rice, and salad of wild greens gathered from the community garden and walked outside to sit at one of the outdoor tables. The sun had set. It was growing dark.

Later on she walked outside, afraid to pursue him. She wandered along the lower path and listened to forest noises. Squirrels and deer and other creatures began to stir as the night darkened. A sliver of moon shone above the trees. She felt so alone.

He felt sorry for her. That was it. Nothing more.

Don't make a big romance over this, she told herself. It's no big deal. He just pitied me.

And he, too, avoided her the next day.

But the next morning, as she wrung out the wet mop on the grass beneath the women's bathroom, he strode towards her.

"Hi, Hannah," he said, as if nothing at all had happened.

"Hi, Sean."

He asked if she would like to take a walk with him when she'd finished her chores. He had binoculars and a guidebook of birds in the region.

Her breath quickened. Oh yes, she cried. But then that

inner voice threatened that she should go home. The police might find her and stick her in a foster home, as her mother had threatened. A home where she would probably be abused and raped. She was bad! She did not deserve a boyfriend!

But she wanted to be with him.

"Okay," she said, feeling numb.

As they walked along the steep path that led up the hill, the tension between them was electric. Every once in a while they stopped to watch a robin or a starling half-hidden in the branches. The touch of his hand when he handed her the binoculars made her tremble. The path wound up to the crest, where once again they sat down beneath the oak tree to rest. He put his arm around her, and she leaned against him, feeling pleasure in the soft air, the sunshine, the feel of his body.

That night as she lay awake, unable to sleep for thinking about him, there was a knock at the door. Her heart pounded. She got out of her sleeping bag, walked over to the door, and opened it. "Come in," she said.

He took her in his arms and kissed her hard on the mouth.

Feeling reckless, she led him back to her sleeping bag. They unzipped it, and all night they held each other, their clothes still on. She could feel his sex hard against her, and she wanted to let him do more, but she was afraid.

Every night that week they lay together. They piled blankets on top of the unzipped bag, and they held each other. The smell of him, the rhythm of his breath, the feel of him against her was overpowering. During the day she wandered around in a semi-daze. He was helping Ted, and on several mornings she and Sean worked together with sheetrock. When no one was looking, he would hold her close and kiss her tenderly.

She stayed for another week, and every night they slept together.

On their last night, feeling bold, she took off her layers of sweaters and let him hold her breasts. He fumbled with the zipper of her jeans, and then with one accord, they both stripped, and in the cold night air, in the darkness, they felt each other's nakedness.

She lay on her back on the flannel lining of the sleeping bag, and passively allowed him to get on top of her.

"I'm a virgin."

"That's okay. I'll be gentle."

"Is it your first time, too?"

"No," he mumbled. "Here now, relax. I won't hurt you."

But it did hurt when he penetrated, and she could feel the fluid run down her legs, and then afterwards he held her very tightly and whispered that he loved her.

Then fear filled her again. Anxiety swept through her. She had to leave him! Something terrible would happen if she did not return home. Her mother's voice was a fierce wind blowing through her.

During the morning *zazen,* she planned how to get home.

At breakfast, everyone's voices sounded in her ears. Sean saved her a place next to him at the dining table. He brought her a plate of pancakes, and she poured herself coffee from the urn.

"Good morning," said Marge. "You look sleepy."

"I didn't sleep much," murmured Hannah. *Can she tell I'm no longer a virgin?*

She could hardly hold the mug of coffee because her hand trembled so much. She felt disconnected from everyone. Then Sean reached out to caress her hand. His touch alone felt real.

After breakfast they walked back together to their sleeping quarters, and she told him that she needed to go home.

"Hannah, don't leave!" he pleaded.

"I have to!"

His eyes looked hurt, wounded. "I have to go," she said. "My mother needs me. She's sick."

"All of a sudden? Now that we've made love?" His voice showed disbelief.

"We fucked!"

"It was love."

"I have to go home."

"You're scared," he said, "Scared of love."

"I have to go," she repeated. *If I don't leave him, something terrible will happen. This happiness is not real.* Gerda's loneliness tore through her. Gerda needed her. She and her mother were one.

He sat down on the floor and watched as she packed her clothing. A black bra from the thrift store in town. Spare panties. An undershirt. A pair of frayed jeans. A T-shirt emblazoned with the Grateful Dead. The grey sweater that had been singed. A hair brush with strands of her dark hair stuck in the bristles. Body lotion. Lipstick. Eye shadow. Deodorant. More bottles all stuffed into a worn backpack from the free box.

He lay down and stretched himself full length over the threshold. "Don't leave, Hannah. Stay here with me."

"I have to go."

He sat up and gripped her tight against him. "Remember, I love you."

"I love you, too."

"Then stay."

"I can't."

Later that day, Ted gave her a ride to the bus stop.

39.

Light shone through the openings in the blinds of Jakob's bedroom. Shivaya could hear the far-off sound of waves as they broke against the shore. He was still asleep. She lay on her side, pressed against the warmth of his body. The curve of his lips and the shape of his brow, as well as the hawk-like nose, reminded her of her father. After a while he stirred, rubbed his eyes, and looked at her with a quizzical expression. "Hey, you," he said. He pulled her close and stroked her breasts. His strong hands stroked the length of her body down to her buttocks and her inner thighs. She quivered with desire as he thrust into her, and she sank into the delicious feel of making love.

It was Sunday morning. Over coffee and croissants at breakfast, he announced that he needed to work on the half-finished sculpture in his studio. Disturbed, she drove back along the coast. At times her vision blurred with tears. She had envisioned a long walk with him along the beach, huddling against him in a fierce wind, eating fish and chips at a seaside restaurant, watching the sun cast a reddish glow as it sank beneath the horizon. Instead, he had abruptly dismissed her as a casual companion. Good for a night of fucking. He said he'd call. Would he visit? Well, he had a lot of work to do just now, and he rarely made it to San Francisco.

When she arrived at the sanctuary of her apartment, she lay down to rest. Hours later she rose, bathed, and put on a silk robe from India embroidered with gold. She prayed at her altar, where she had lit a candle. She prayed to the Goddess for relief from the ache of wanting love so much. Men had betrayed her! So many men. The three husbands in her past receded into ghostly shadows in light of the present.

She took a photo from her purse that she had hastily snatched from Jakob's bureau when he was in the kitchen. It showed a frail-looking woman with Jakob. His arm rested around her, just above her breast. They looked as if they were in love. She gazed at it a long time. Sobs rose in her throat.

Then she rose, went to her desk, and took out a pair of sharp scissors. Her hand trembled as she cut away the image of the woman, leaving Jakob with his windswept hair, his haunting smile, and his arm in mid-air. She placed the shiny paper of the woman in an ashtray, and she watched as the flame slowly transformed her into ashes. She scooped up the ashes with her fingers and flushed them down the toilet. Then she pasted a photo of herself in that hollow space, so that his arm now rested around her.

It was wrong, she told her students, to force your will upon another person. Yet this is what she was doing. Would he miss the photo and suspect her? Too late now to take it back. Breathe. Send her roots deep into the earth. Picture his energy entwined with hers, crystal-light strands connecting their chakras.

Afterwards she lay down to soothe her aura as well as his, far off in Santa Cruz. She tried, too, to soothe the woman's aura, for surely the woman must sense what had happened. *Shivaya,* whispered a voice as she soared through the night. Whose voice? She had ventured into a realm of questionable spirits. Was it truly the Mother's voice or a voice less benign? She kept on soaring south, her wings spread against the darkness, until the coast receded and she was flying beneath a dark starry sky.

40.

Three people waited in the therapist's office in downtown Berkeley. The first was a stocky man of average height with a compact build. The woman had wild blonde hair. Her chin jutted out. Her features were compelling. They would have magnetized an observer. A drama seemed to be going on each instant within her. Her face and body would pull on an observer. When she spoke, at times her sharp voice had that same magnetic frequency, a vibration that drew the listener closer.

Don't hang up on me.

Listen.

Help.

This woman spent hours each day on her phone, TV sound turned down, its silent images floating in front of her eyes as she held the receiver to her ear and spoke to an invisible listener.

The third figure was a young girl of fourteen, with her father's black curls. She was the estranged couple's daughter.

Saul, Gerda, and Hannah.

"We've been through this so many times in the past few weeks," thought the man. Sad. Sinking. In the back of his mind floated lists of groceries to buy, work to do at the Lab, a paper to revise, along with a wave of anger as he looked at Hannah and Gerda, his former wife. Strange to think he and Gerda had once shared a bed, that for years their lives had been entirely entwined. *Poor kid. Her fault? They've got you by the balls. Buy them. Buy those balls.* Nonsensical words ran through his mind.

He glanced at his watch. The woman glanced at her more delicate watch with its thin leather band. She, too, had a list running through her mind. Pills to take on schedule. A sale at the local thrift shop. Her coffee date with Barbara this afternoon. She needed to buy Adam more clothing at J.C. Penney. Esther's teacher wanted to see her. She dreaded that meeting! The girl, Hannah, stared straight ahead, dressed in the jeans and faded pink T-shirt she had worn every day since coming home.

The psychiatrist walked in, barrel-chested, wearing black T-shirt, Levis, and tooled leather boots. His hair was grey, and he was partially bald.

Voices.

The girl listened to the voices. *They will never get me to talk.*

"She is controlling us," said the woman.

Boundaries.

Her parents' energy filled her up. She wanted to scream, cover her ears with her hands, and jump out the window, which was on the second floor of this ultra-modern, sterile office building.

Too much pain.

Dad's lonely apartment.

Too much pain. So I left. But they brought me back into hell.

They are talking now about Shivaya. Who cares? Fuck Shivaya. Take away her papers. Arrest her. Shit. Don't hurt Shivaya. She only tried to help me. I begged her to take me away.

Words stuck in the girl's throat. She could not speak. Her tongue, her mouth, her throat were paralyzed.

Her father was shaking her shoulders.

Talk, they begged her.

"Goddamn you! I'll never get well!"

She barely heard her own words. It was as if someone else had spoken,

Afterwards the man and woman drove home separately.

The girl was silent in her father's car.

Cars.

Speed.

Broken white lines.

Stay within the correct lane. Don't get killed. So easy to die.

The man's hand stiffened over the steering wheel, as if he sensed the girl's thoughts. The roll of flesh over his shoulders grew imperceptibly thicker. A strong wind was blowing, and he had to keep the car from swerving.

The woman, who was driving a heavier car, kept it steady against the force of the wind while she hastened home, where she would phone Barbara. A voice to fill the void. A sympathetic listener.

The girl began to sweat. She watched her Dad. The set of his jaw was rigid. *No one knows how I hurt.* Her hands were shaking from too much caffeine. Yellow line in the center of the road. Oncoming traffic. So easy to die! She lurched forward and gripped the steering wheel, cold and thick to the touch.

His right arm shot out, hurling her against the passenger door.

She screamed.

The wind blew harder against the sound of her cries.

41.

If only he could help her. But it was as if a block of ice imprisoned him, and he could not find words to express to her the love he had for her. She was breaking his heart. If only he could let her know how much he loved her.

Why did he blow up at the poor kid? She had been silent most of the time she'd been with him in his cramped one-bedroom apartment. His darling Hannah. Slept on a mattress in the middle of the living room floor so that he had to step over her in the morning when he got up to make breakfast. She lay there, obstructing his path as he attempted to walk through the living room to the kitchen and to the front door, which opened onto an outdoor corridor and the steps leading down to the parking lot.

It was a grim and cheap little apartment. He missed their old house. Poor kid. "She's possessed," said Gerda. It was ironic, he thought, for *her,* the skeptic, to make such a remark. "Why the hell did Shivaya take her to the mountains?" In truth, something had harmed Hannah. Something beyond him or Gerda. Something had deeply harmed and altered her.

Hannah, speak to me.

In his dreams, she was weeping.

Wise men with cloud-like faces surrounded him in his dream. He wanted to see their features. Why were they concealing themselves?

"I hate you, Daddy!" she screamed.

Who screamed?

The voice screamed through her.

See here, Mom, now I have a voice riding me just like you do.

"Asshole!"

Saul turned on his heels and walked away from her into the kitchen, while she pounded her fists against the floor and kicked her feet like a two-year-old.

"Don't talk that way!" he shouted. There was a hard knot inside him. *You do have a devil inside you—just like your mother,* he wanted to say, barely restraining himself, biting his lips to keep from speaking aloud. His body grew more rigid as he walked stiffly around the tiny kitchen. He washed the blue and white Formica breakfast dishes that were coated with congealed egg, dried them, heated water for instant coffee, emptied the sink drain of gunk, checked the thermostat in the living room. Hannah had set it too high.

"Eighty degrees!" he shouted. "Are you crazy? Our gas bill will go through the roof."

"Oh, Dad," she scoffed. "Penny pinching."

"Well, damn it, who earns the money? What do you do all day but lie here and do nothing?"

"Asshole!"

He walked outside, slamming the door behind him, and sat on the hard metal chair on the narrow porch to smoke his pipe. Ah, the good smell of the tobacco. His father, too, had smoked a pipe, and this thought comforted him.

Something as hard as ice, as molten as lava, alternately froze and burned inside him. He could not reach down and smooth her hair, embrace her, soothe her anguish, could not say, "I understand. I love you."

Flashback. His mother and his grandmother were placing a long tube over his body as he lay sick in bed. Inside the tube were hot electric lights. He was five years old. He feared they had turned into witches, and that they were going to kill him.

"Is there a devil inside you, Hannah?" he yelled one night.

"Yes," she said. "Maybe there is."

The voice spoke louder. Each day Hannah continued her retreat from the world. She would lie asleep on the mattress long after Saul had left for work. It had been months since she attended school, and her teachers assumed that she was no longer enrolled.

One day when she was alone, she sat down on the floor and lit a match. She watched it glow until it singed her fingers. Then she tossed it down, still burning on the carpet. It died, leaving a dark scorched blotch. She struck another match. Watched the flame glow in hues that shifted like waves. Her eyes glazed over as she watched, spell-bound, ignoring the pain when it licked her fingers. This time she would feed its flame with scraps of paper and set the whole apartment ablaze.

Just then the phone rang. With a start, she blew out the flame. *Don't answer. Let the damned phone ring on and on.*

42.

With all the family troubles weighing on him, Saul had not contacted Shivaya since his return from Frankfurt. Yet one Thursday evening he waited outside in his car until he saw the last of her students leave. Then he climbed the stairs of her building and knocked on her door.

"Saul!" She looked startled. Her face was unusually pale, with feverish splotches of red on her cheeks. She was wearing loose harem pants of gauzy blue material along with a tank top, and she was barefoot.

"Come in," she said, recovering her poise.

"Thank you." He entered the familiar living room with its lingering scent of rose oil.

"Saul, it's good to see you. But you might have called first."

He cleared his throat. How to say what he needed to say? "I'm sorry. I should have called. I need to talk with you."

"Sit down. I'll make you a cup of tea or something stronger if you like."

"No thanks."

"Sit down," she repeated. "I'll be back in a minute."

She went into the bathroom to collect her thoughts.

How to tell him about Jakob? That she had fallen in love with Jakob. But Saul was obviously in pain. She needed to be gentle with him. She brushed her hair and mentally smoothed her aura as the brush swept through her hair. She applied fresh lipstick—a kind of armor—and returned to the living room. He was sitting stiffly on the sofa. He looked up at her and said in a taut voice that Hannah was in a desperate state. "She's been a wreck ever since she returned from the mountains."

"Hannah should never have come back," said Shivaya. She sat down on the carpet by the sofa. "Saul, she was happy there." She looked up at him with her clear grey eyes. "She'd met a boy she liked. She called me once, all excited and happy about him, and she loved being there."

"Then why did she come back so miserable?"

"Saul, we've talked about psychically binding a person to you. Invisible extensions of energy. Gerda was clutching at Hannah, digging into her chakras so that Hannah could no longer think straight. Gerda's energy overpowered her. Hannah felt absolutely compelled to return, although she didn't know why. She felt Gerda's pain as if it were her own, and because she is a loving soul, she returned."

"I don't understand."

"I think you do, Saul. We've talked about all this, and we've worked with it in class."

In his heart he did understand. His dreams contained images from which he shrank. Images of corpses strewn on bare rocky terrain. "Every time I look at her," he said, "It tears me apart. Sometime I wish I could shoot her like a horse with a broken leg to relieve her pain. She's broken."

"Don't say that! Don't even think that! She's not broken, but she's hurting a lot."

In spite of his attempts to hold back, he found himself sobbing.

She raised herself up, put her arms around him, and held him close. Her fragrance and the softness of her breasts aroused him.

"Shivaya, I want to make love to you," he whispered.

She drew back from his caress. "Saul, I can't." She paused, thinking of how to say it without hurting him, but there was no way she could. "While you were gone, I met someone." Her voice faltered.

"Who is he?"

"Another Dane. An artist. We met in Santa Cruz."

"I see."

His expression, so crushed, filled her with pity. She drew close again and held him. "I still care for you very much, and I always will."

He wrenched away . "Shivaya, just leave me alone!"

He stood up abruptly and walked quickly out the door before she could stop him.

43.

It hurt Esther to see her sister act so mean to Dad. Poor Dad who worked so hard. "I don't know how to handle her," said Saul. He and Esther were walking home from Safeway with bags of groceries in their arms. She liked to help him shop and liked to help clean the small apartment.

On weekends she and Adam joined their sister at their Dad's. She sometimes fantasized that Adam was really her child. During the long weekends at their Dad's she made sure his toys were there. She listened to him when no one else did. He was now two and a half, and he had begun to scream in frustration if his desires were thwarted. "Ice cream! I want ice cream! My truck! My red truck!" She learned to divert him with games like hide and seek or a version of Simon Says. (Effective for getting him to pick up his toys!) Hannah also played with him and gave him affectionate hugs when she was aware of anything outside her own suffering.

"You're doing the best you can, Dad," Esther said as they walked along the narrow sidewalk. The bag felt so heavy in her arms.

All those weeks when Hannah had been away at Enkoji, she had missed her. It had been lonely at night without Hannah in the other twin bed at their Mom's, and it still was, now that Hannah lived with their Dad. She sorely missed her sister, but knowing of Hannah's unhappiness, she could understand why she had fled. She had hoped all during that time that her sister was okay, the sister who had bossed her around, whom at times Esther had hated. But now that she was gone, it was as if part of her own self were missing. The big white bureau was still filled with her clothes. Her photos of friends still stood on top of the bureau; her shoes remained in the closet. Esther even missed Hannah's messiness, her habit of leaving clothes heaped in piles on the floor. She missed the scent of Hannah in the room, missed their whispered talks at night.

But Hannah had changed. Esther felt bereft. A chasm separated them. So much was inside Esther, she felt at times as if she would burst, but she focused on holding it all in, deep darkness inside her like a well. It gave her strength.

Her father had a dark well, too, shielded by walls of steel. His source lay deeper inside him, almost hidden even from himself. She felt that she understood him in a way that no one else did. She understood the tender self hidden deep inside him, the loving tender father self. She saw how it hurt him, breaking up as he had with Shivaya. She had never liked the woman, but Shivaya had made him happier for a while.

At thirteen, Esther had become a woman. Fully developed. Careful of how she dressed, of how she presented herself to others. A woman with breasts and hips. She applied lipstick, mascara and eyeliner each morning before she went to school or stepped out into the world.

Hannah didn't care as much about how she looked. Hannah was hotheaded and impetuous. Circumspect by nature, Esther had become more so as she saw how it wounded Hannah to hurl herself against her parents. Unlike Hannah, she took her mother's scoldings and physical abuse with silent stoicism.

Then there was Dominic.

A thin, intense boy from her algebra class who would meet her in the apartment parking lot, where he waited outside in his 1966 Ford. They made out in deserted spots in the hills and at other times in the darkness of the back row of the movie theater. To feel his hands move over her body, to feel him taut and throbbing, gave her a rebellious kind of satisfaction which both aroused and comforted her.

44.

Hannah moved quietly so as not to wake Esther in the darkness. She stumbled over her pillow on the floor. She gathered the backpack she had filled earlier, her purse, and her shoes, which she carried in her hands as she quietly opened the door of the apartment and walked down the steps. Stars still shone in the sky. It was cold. She wrapped her jacket more tightly around her. The first BART train of the day took her to the Greyhound terminal in downtown Oakland. There were only a few passengers on the bus. She placed her pack in the overhead rack and sat down next to a window. The torn plastic seat felt slippery beneath her. Across the aisle sat an old woman in a ragged purple cardigan who was praying under her breath in Spanish. Two men in the back of the bus were drinking from bottles in paper bags, and she smelled a whiff of alcohol. As the bus drove south on the freeway, the dark sky began to lighten into morning.

She dozed off and on, lulled by the motion of the vehicle, until the bus driver's loud voice woke her as he called out, "Last stop." They were in front of a Safeway grocery. She recognized the store, the buildings, and the phone booth across the street which had been the scene of her anguished calls to her mother.

She heaved her backpack onto her shoulders and walked beyond the outskirts of the town, onto a narrow road that wound uphill through woods and trees. After a while she stopped to rest beneath a pine tree. The ground was cold and damp. Clouds had gathered in the sky. A plump woman in a dark station wagon stopped and got out. She wore tight jeans, a bulky sweater, and a hiker's headscarf. "Are you all right?" she asked.

"I'm okay," said Hannah. "I'm on my way to Enkoji."

"I know the place," said the woman. "Come on, I'll give you a lift."

"Thanks," said Hannah. The woman had a kind face. She seemed safe.

In the back seat of the station wagon was a sheep dog with mottled blond fur. Hannah reached back and tentatively extended her palm. The dog licked it, and she patted its fur.

"He's very friendly," said the woman, whose voice had a cheerful lift.

They drove on.

At the entrance to the deep road that led to Enkoji, Hannah got out. "Will you be all right?" said the woman. "Yes," said Hannah. As the car drove off, a jolt of fear shot through her. She lifted the backpack and adjusted it behind her back. It felt heavier than before. The sun, a red globe, sank lower in the sky behind the hills as she walked down the steep slope. She walked with slow steady steps to keep her balance.

45.

"Shivaya has changed," said her students.

She seemed on edge. At times her voice trembled; and she was harsh in a way that she had never been before, particularly with a young woman in her Thursday class who sobbed afterwards and never returned.

She took up smoking again, after years of abstinence. Marlboros.

Jakob. Her world whirled around him as its center, nebulous figure that he was. She needed him as desperately as she needed food or water.

One Friday in December he called and asked to visit her.

She floated around her apartment in a state of anticipation. This would be his first visit! The magic was working: the visualization, the binding of his energy with hers, the spell she had found in an ancient book on Celtic witchcraft among her collection of occult literature.

He rang the doorbell shortly after dusk. In his arms he held a potted scarlet poinsettia plant. His face was ruddy with cold. He had on the soft suede jacket that she loved, along with jeans, a sweater, and brogans.

"Come in."

She tried to embrace him, but he felt stiff, and the poinsettia was between them.

"Hello, *Katrina,*" he said, emphasizing it. *Her real name.* And he stepped inside.

"Nice place you have." He set the poinsettia down on a small table and looked around the living room with its rich green carpet, the grey sofa and matching armchair, the folding metal chairs stacked in a corner for her students, and the Japanese screen that partially concealed her altar.

"It's so warm in here."

"Too warm?"

"I like it colder."

"I keep it warm for stretching and yoga. I suppose I'm more sensitive to cold than you."

He paced back and forth.

"Would you like to see the rest of the apartment?"

"No, that's okay."

"How about a drink?"

"Do you have any beer?"

"I do."

While he examined her collection of books, she took the plant into the kitchen and came back with two bottles of Dos Equis and two tall Mexican glasses with blue rims. He drank his beer straight from the bottle, scorning the glass, and she sensed that something was terribly wrong. She poured her own beer into a glass and took a sip.

"You look so serious."

"I am," he said, and he looked straight into her eyes. She knew that he sensed what she had done. He took her hand, which felt cold, into his large warm calloused hand and fingered her palm with his thumb.

"I can feel . . . what can I say . . . how can I . . . I'm sensitive to energy, like you are . . . I can feel how serious you are about me. You want more from me, more than I can give . . . I've been with a woman now for eight years . . . She's in England right now, she's been visiting her family . . . and I'm committed to her . . . I can't give you what you want . . . "

Karma. She had wounded Saul. Her turn now to feel the knife.

"I see you have a collection of books on magic and esoteric subjects. Perhaps you think you can work some kind of magic, but it won't work. "

Did he know about the photo? He didn't mention it, but she knew he knew.

"I think we'd better break this off before it goes further," he said in a gentle voice. He still held her hand, but he looked away.

"I see," she said. More words would not come. She felt frozen. Her soulmate. He was her soulmate, and he clairvoyantly sensed what she had done. He did not need to mention the missing photo, but he knew.

"It's better if we break it off now. Before either of us gets entangled. Katrina, I could easily fall in love with you. But I've built a life with Elsa. It's better if we don't see each other. If we just cut it off now."

Echoes of her father. A cold rainy day in Copenhagen. She was with her father in a crowded café. His white hair added to his air of distinction. He wore a suede jacket like Jakob's over a black sweater and black cashmere scarf.

"Your mother was so needy. So desperate for love that I couldn't stand it," he told her. "I had no energy for creative work. My poetry vanished under the weight of her desperation for me to give more than I could possibly give. I couldn't stand her patient suffering. I acted in cruel ways, but I had to leave."

Now tears welled up; she struggled to hold back sobs. "You're okay, baby," he said and he took her into his arms for what she knew would be the last time.

After he left, she lit a candle, burned incense, and lay down in her bed. When she woke up, it was early evening, and the setting sun cast an oblique light through the blinds.

The next day she cleaned the apartment, washed her hair, and threw out the poinsettia plant. That night she taught her class with unusual calm.

46.
January, 1977

Hannah vomited into the toilet bowl. Then she straightened up, took hold of the mop, and continued mopping the linoleum. But the nausea surged up again. She leaned the mop handle against the wall with its poster of a bird in flight, and she rushed once again to the toilet. This morning's oatmeal erupted along with orange juice. She hoped no one had heard her vomit. She didn't want them to know! Not yet. Maybe she was just sick? Maybe it was just nerves that had delayed her period for so long and made her feel this way.

She flushed the toilet. Closed the lid. Sat down on the seat until the dizziness passed. Then she got up, rinsed her mouth, and washed her hands at the sink. She wrung out the cold mop in her bare hands and continued her work.

On the wall of the women's bathroom hung a square piece of vellum paper with Japanese black calligraphy alongside the English words. *Be peaceful. Be mindful. Do no harm.*

No harm? No harm if she wasn't pregnant. No harm to kill the blob inside her if she was? She thought of Adam's soft spot. The day she'd looked down on him as he slept and thought about smashing his skull. But she hadn't touched him. Instead, she had tiptoed softly out of the room.

Footsteps sounded. The outside door opened, and Marge walked in, flushed from the cold. "Are you all right?" she asked. "I heard you vomiting."

"I'm okay."

"You don't look well. You're pale."

Hannah bit her lips then blurted, "I'm pregnant."

"What?" Marge's expression changed. She looked at Hannah for a moment of frightening silence.

"Are you sure?"

"I haven't had my period in two months."

"Have you had a pregnancy test?"

"No. But I'm sure. I can feel it."

"Well, you need to get tested. I'll take you to a clinic."

"If I am pregnant, can I stay?"

Marge sighed. "We'll see." She smoothed Hannah's forehead, and Hannah burst into tears. Marge hugged her and stroked her shoulders in a way that felt comforting. "Things have a way of working out," she said. "Now let's get on with our chores. Finish the bathroom, and come and help me sew curtains."

After she'd helped with the curtains, Hannah walked outside into the crisp morning air with its smell of wood smoke. Would they let her stay? The idea of going home felt like snakes wrapping around her throat. Better to have an abortion. Better to have the baby alone on the street!

A few flakes of snow began to drift down from the white wintry sky. She stood there in the cold, transfixed by her thoughts. It began to snow harder, covering her face and shoulders with a glistening white mantle of large wet flakes that immediately melted.

When the meeting began, Hannah walked up the hill to quiet her tension. At the crest she could see the Bay far below, glistening beneath the sun, where it touched the far-off haze of sky. She walked along the crest trail and kicked stones beneath her feet. A rabbit scooted in front of her. A skinny grey rabbit. So sweet. She longed to run after it, catch it, and keep it in her cabin as a pet. There were rustlings in the underbrush of other forest animals, too shy to appear during the day. Too shy or frightened or perhaps too wise. At night the deer came out, as well as rabbits, skunks, raccoons, and occasional bears during the dry season. A squirrel scuttled up a tree. In the distance two ravens circled over a carcass hidden in a hollow. She kept on walking. The sun rose higher. She took off her jacket and tied it around her waist. Kept on walking.

Later, too tense to eat lunch, she crept into the kitchen where she could listen, unobserved and hidden. Marge had told her to wait until the end of the meeting to speak her piece. She could hear their voices through the wall.

"What if there are complications?" said Molly. "We're far from any medical facilities. In Santa Cruz, she can get help. Aid to women with dependent children. Food stamps. Welfare. Social workers."

"She would hate that!" said Ted.

Thank God for Ted! If only Sean were here! Hannah had no idea where he was. She had written to him at his parents' address, but there was no answer.

"She wants to stay," said Marge.

"No!" cried Sergio. "This is a spiritual retreat! Not a home for unwed mothers."

"She can put up the baby for adoption."

Hannah could hold back no longer. She burst into the living room and cried, "I'm keeping the baby! It's Sean's baby, too!"

"Don't count on him," said Marge.

"I'll raise the baby alone."

"You'd be better off going home."

"No!" she cried. "You don't understand!"

"What would Hakuin do?" asked Ted.

Silence.

"He would let her stay," said Marge in a quiet voice.

The air shifted. Hannah could feel molecules shift around her and inside her body.

"Okay with me, I guess. We can all give a little. Poor kid!" said Joe. He wiped his whiskers.

"What do the rest of you think?"

"It's not okay!" cried Sergio. His chin quivered. His dark eyes flashed in rage. "If she stays, I leave."

"She's staying," said Ted.

Sergio stood up, pounded his chair against the floor, and stomped out of the room.

Everyone was silent for a moment.

"I never did like that guy," Ted said at last.

"Oh God, I'm sorry," said Hannah. She stiffened and clenched her fists. "I've created an awful situation. I should leave."

"No, you stay," said Marge. She and Molly put their arms around her, and then Ted did, too. Finally Joe, casting aside his cane, embraced them all. Surrounded as she was, feeling their bodies close, she wanted to cry. Her family! At least for now.

47.

The ringing phone woke him from a dream where he was walking somewhere with Hannah. Drowsily, he reached for the phone.

"Esther told me what happened. Why didn't you tell me?"

"Gerda, it's six o'clock in the morning . . ."

"I'm sorry I woke you. We've got to talk to Shivaya. She's responsible."

"She won't be up yet, and I have to go to work."

"Fuck your work. This is more important. I don't want to give her any warning!"

Useless to argue. That sharp voice would go on and on. Save his strength for later. Instead he called the Lab to say that he would be late, made himself toast and coffee, and meditated in order to compose himself. He looked down at his hands. Hairy, muscular, squat hands. He had read about lucid dreaming. The first step in gaining control was to look at your hands inside the dream. The next step was teleportation. If he could learn to do that, perhaps he could watch over Hannah and protect her from danger.

At nine o'clock that morning he and Gerda settled

themselves awkwardly on the sofa in Shivaya's living room while she faced them in an armchair, her legs folded beneath her, and gripped her warm mug of coffee for comfort. She wore a white silk kimono with gold embroidery. No underwear, thought Gerda, who could see a hint of Shivaya's pale thighs. There was the scent of sandalwood incense. A bronze Buddha gazed at them from the corner.

"She wanted very much to go back," Shivaya said.

"You pushed her," said Gerda.

"I showed her a place of refuge."

"She doesn't belong there. She's only fifteen. She should be in school."

"She was on the edge of suicide. She obsessed about slitting her wrists. She phoned me in desperation."

"I don't believe you," said Gerda. "Hannah was never suicidal."

"How little you know your own daughter. Things were terrible for her at home. You both caused her a lot of suffering."

"Not true!" cried Gerda. "We had our moments, but Hannah and I love each other. We have a good relationship. Mothers and daughters always fight. She's at that rebellious adolescent stage. She was fine until you kidnapped her. I will report you to Immigration."

"No, you won't." Saul stood up, and his compact, stocky body exuded flames from its aura. "Gerda, you have a history of mental illness. Certifiable." Shivaya watched, fascinated. She had never seen him so angry. "Shivaya has done nothing wrong. She stretched out a hand to help Hannah when we couldn't."

"I'll have the police bring her back."

Shivaya took a deep breath and plunged. "She's pregnant."

Both parents were silent.

Then Gerda said, "She's too young to have a baby. She needs to come home!"

"Let her be," said Saul, although the revelation that his daughter was pregnant sent a shock through his body.

Shivaya's bones and muscles sagged. She felt in that instant many years older. The glamorous blonde Nordic was giving way to a tired, pale middle-aged woman. An ordinary woman, despite the silk kimono with its gold embroidery and the black velveteen slippers.

She gathered her strength. "Hannah is safe," she said. "Hannah is doing what she has to in order to survive." She looked down at the carpet. Her toe nail polish, blood red, was too harsh. The image of fire came to mind. "Hannah wanted to set the apartment on fire," she said in a low voice. "She thought about setting her hair on fire."

"She did set a fire once," said Saul.

"She's with good people now at Enkoji. They like her, and they accept her as she is."

"Who lives there? Hippies on drugs? Is she fucking everyone in sight? Whose baby is this? Does she have any idea? It could be a drug-addicted baby."

"They're good people," Shivaya repeated. "No drugs. Trees. Earth. Water. Sky. Meditation. Good energy!"

"Shivaya, you are all airy fairy. Feet above the earth. You're the reason Saul left us!"

"Just shut up," cried Saul.

"Hannah is safe," Shivaya repeated.

"Who are you to know what's good for Hannah? You

are a whore! Just a whore selling this New Age shit and pretending to be so enlightened!"

Saul raised a threatening hand.

"Don't hit me!"

Yin and yang, thought Shivaya, as she saw how their auras connected and inflamed each other.

"That's enough," Shivaya said quietly. She sent out grounding waves of energy.

The room grew silent. Only the ticking of a clock sounded. The Buddha gazed at them impassively from the corner. The smell of incense grew stronger.

Shivaya rose, walked to the door, and opened it. "Go," she said. "Just go. Go in peace."

That night, Saul realized he was dreaming as he floated invisibly over Hannah to let her know that he loved her. At that moment Shivaya, in trance, took the form of a gull and spread her wings. She swooped down into Gerda's heart, and what she saw filled her with a sense of urgency.

48.

Gerda slept fitfully and woke up while it was still dark. She began to fumble through Hannah's bureau while Esther, still half asleep, stirred in her bed. "Mom," she murmured, anxiously.

"Go back to sleep!" barked Gerda. Here were old worn cotton underpants, undershirts from when she was younger, two bras, six T-shirts, three warm sweaters from the closet, two pairs of heavy jeans for cold. One was flannel-lined from two years ago, when Hannah's class had taken a trip to the Sierras in winter. The old rust-colored down jacket from last winter. Socks … where were they? Ah, here . . . three pairs of Esther's socks would do . . . and Hannah's worn leather boots with the Western cowboy-like imprints.

She stuffed the clothing into a laundry bag and flung it onto the back seat of her car. Put the boots on the car floor. Then she made herself a cup of coffee. Drank it black and bitter, no sugar or cream. Scribbled a note for Esther and left it on the kitchen table. Just as she was putting on her jacket in the hallway, Esther padded into view, her face still puffy with sleep.

"Mom, what's going on?"

"I have to get Hannah."

"Why? What happened?"

"I have to get her home."

"Why?"

"Esther, just leave me alone."

"Tell me, what's going on? Is she okay?"

"I don't have time to talk!" Her hands trembled as she tried to zip up her jacket.

"Oh, Mom . . . " Esther swallowed and kept silent, determined to call her father the moment her mother left the house.

She had to get Hannah home! That thought completely filled Gerda's mind. Hannah was too young to have a baby all alone. She needed care. Perhaps an abortion or an adoption would be the solution . . . Oh, the shame of it! A pregnant, unmarried daughter, not yet even sixteen years old. They'd keep it quiet. No need to let people know. Hippies! All that Buddhist bullshit was only a cover, she was sure, for lazy, drugged lives. She had to free Hannah from their influence.

Her hands trembled on the wheel. She was driving south on 880. It was a cold, grey morning. The weather report predicted snow in the Sierras. Rain began falling. The drops turned into hard lumps of hail hitting the windshield, then back again into rain that began to fall in torrents, obscuring her vision. The rear defogger did not work.

She had to bring her child home. This thought obliterated all else. She had an image of Hannah lying on a filthy mattress and moaning with labor pains. Other images flashed through her mind: a bearded man with eyes as hard as stone was raping her while she lay spread eagled on concrete, her hands tied above her head. Hannah weeping as she fought her way through a tangled forest undergrowth to escape them all.

She had to free her daughter! Take her home. Protect her. Guide her because she was far too young to guide herself. She would take care of Hannah and Hannah's child, and Hannah would never leave her.

A siren sounded. When she looked into the rearview mirror she saw the flashing lights of a police car. She skidded to a stop. After what seemed hours but were only minutes, a police officer got out of the vehicle and came towards her. She rolled down her window. Her hands felt stiff.

"Ma'am, do you know how fast you were going?"

"No, Officer."

"Nearly eighty."

In a daze, she handed him her license and registration. In spite of the cold rain falling, he wrote out a ticket with nerve-racking deliberation.

"Watch it now, Ma'am. The roads are slippery with rain and ice."

Although it was mid-morning, the sky had turned dark, and the falling rain obscured her view. The wipers made a scraping noise as they moved across the windshield.

Where was the turnoff? She had written it down, but in her jumbled mind she could not remember where it was. Perhaps they planned to sacrifice her. She visualized Hannah in a white robe, tied to a stake.

The rain kept coming down hard, and it was difficult to see ahead. The wipers moved back and forth in a hypnotic and maddening motion. The rear window was entirely fogged up.

Could Hannah possibly not be Saul's? Had she, Gerda, unknowingly been unfaithful? One night she'd gone with a man for a few drinks after her TESL class. Could she have let the memory of what happened slip her mind? The man merged into an image of her father. Crazy thoughts! Hannah had come out of her own womb. Fragments of a dream.

Crazy dream.

Saul and Shivaya were in league against her. They were still sleeping together. She could tell by the way Shivaya touched Saul's hand when they walked in. Shivaya had probably given Hannah drugs!

She, Gerda, had to get there in time.

Crazy thoughts.

Where was her mind? What was real? This highway stretching in front of her.

Hannah is too young to have a baby. I will contact an adoption agency. I will send her to a home for unwed mothers and arrange for the adoption.

Hannah would stay with her forever. Hannah would care for Gerda in her old age, while Adam and Esther might desert her. But Hannah was special. Hannah was hers alone.

They are plotting to enslave Hannah in their cult. I will call Children's Protective Services. I will contact Immigration about Shivaya and have them deport her. I will make Saul suffer for the rest of his life for all that he has done to us. I will have the authorities shut down that hippie commune.

The stretch of highway ahead became a blur. The wipers scraping against the windshield were hypnotic, abrasive. She trembled as she pressed her foot down harder on the gas pedal. *Faster. Go faster.*

She didn't see the truck looming towards her from the opposite lane until it was too late. Too late to slam on the brakes, too late before the crash, the splintering of glass and metal, the rolling forward, and then darkness.

49.

"The phone lines have gone down," said Ted. "Sean tried to call, but he got cut off."

The electricity, too, had gone out. They were eating dinner in the kitchen by the light of a kerosene lamp, where the gas stove gave off a little heat.

"Does he know I'm pregnant?" asked Hannah.

Ted and Marge exchanged glances. Marge then looked directly at Hannah. "I told him. I thought it was best."

"I hope that doesn't scare him away." Hannah stared down at her beans and rice. They seemed immense in the pile on her plate, too much to digest.

"It's his problem, honey, not yours."

"We're here for you," said Ted. He moved his chair closer to Hannah and put his arm around her. "You've got us. We're family."

"I'm thankful to all of you," said Hannah. She forced herself to smile. She wished Sean were here. She ached for him.

They finished eating, cleared the plates, and Hannah sponged off the table. She filled a large thermos with hot tea to take with her for the night, went to the bathroom to brush her teeth and splash cold water on her face, then walked back to her cabin.

Snowflakes fell on her face and clothing as she walked along the path. A shaft of moonlight shone through the clouds. The strong winds earlier had not only downed utility lines but left broken-off tree branches and leaves in their wake.

Inside the cabin she put a pine log in the stove, lit it under a pile of newspapers, and watched it blaze. She took off her clothing, and naked, shivering in the cold, slipped into her flannel nightgown and thick woolen socks. For a while she crouched in front of the stove and watched its flames, ever-changing and hypnotic. She imagined walking into the flames and into a different world, a world that did not burn but glowed orange and red and deep blue as it revealed mysterious caves and passageways.

A wave of darkness swept through her. Something had happened to her mother. She could sense it, but she felt powerless. "You are breaking my heart," her mother had said this morning when she phoned and got through to Enkoji just before the storm. Her mother's voice had a tone that Hannah had never heard before.

She had to stand firm against her mother's words. If she went home, she would not be strong enough. She had to be strong for this fragile life inside her.

"You're stronger than you think," Shivaya had told her.

"We're here for you," Marge and Ted had said.

Thank God for them. God had brought them into her life, said Shivaya, who rarely spoke of God. Shivaya had woven these people into her life.

She inhaled the smoky odor of the burning pine. Flames cast shadows on the walls. She grew drowsy and lay down on her narrow bed with its layers of blankets and soft, warm goose-down quilt. How cozy it was to lie here in the semi-darkness and watch the flames light the room with a dancing, ever-changing motion. Her clothing hung on hooks on the wall and in neatly folded piles on wooden crate shelves. Her shoes lined up by the door. She had fallen half asleep when she heard loud knocks.

"Can I come in?" Sean's voice.

A thrill ran through her. "Yes," she said.

He entered, bringing with him a gust of cold air. She sat up and hugged her arms to her chest. He was carrying a heavy backpack and a guitar case flecked with snow. He set them down, took off his jacket and boots, then sat down beside her on the bed. He caressed her cheek and patted her stomach.

"You know," she said.

"Yes," he said. "I know. Is it mine?"

"Sean, I've made love once in my entire life and it was with you."

"What about the time we were apart?"

She looked into his eyes. "There was no one else. You're the father."

"Wow!" He took a deep breath.

"What are you going to do?"

"I'm going to have the baby."

"It was an accident . . . the pregnancy . . . I'm not ready for this."

"The baby is ready. Babies don't wait."

He gripped her cold hands. His large hands felt warmer. His fingers were long and thin. A musician's hands, she thought. He drew her close. "Hannah, I love you. I've thought a lot about you." He paused. "I've dropped out of school. I joined a rock band. In the spring we're going to Europe. I don't know how long I'll be away."

"I'm glad for you." She forced herself to smile.

He stood up and put a log on the fire. His face glowed in the glare of the flames. "I can't promise you anything ... It's only been a couple of months, right?" His speech quickened. "I'll pay for an abortion."

"I don't want one."

"If you change your mind, there's still time."

"No!" She burst into tears.

He held her close, wiped her tears. She hid her face in the rough texture of his sweater. Looked up at his face. He was trembling. Then he pulled her down onto the bed. She could feel his sex hard against her. She throbbed with wanting him. He pushed her nightgown up above her thighs, fumbled with his clothing, made love to her. All night they held each other, naked beneath the warmth of the thick quilt. Her legs wrapped around him, as if in this way she could hold him forever.

With the first dawn light he rose, dressed, leaned down over her, and kissed her goodbye. Then he heaved his backpack and guitar case onto his shoulders and walked out the door, briefly letting in a blast of cold air.

Later that day she walked up the steep path that led to a clearing at the top of the crest. All around her were rocks and wild dry grass, lightly covered with snow. She looked down at the ocean. Its dark water paled until it merged with the sky. She felt Shivaya's strength flowing through her. She was nearly in her third month. Soon this creature inside her would begin to move.

50.

For three days Gerda lay in intensive care at San Jose Kaiser Hospital with tubes attached to her body. Heavy sedation reduced the pain, but she could feel nothing in her legs, and she could not move them. In and out of consciousness she drifted, but mostly she slept. Visions. Memories. Real or unreal? The pink blanket. The bricks falling all around her. Her mother and father, youthful as they had been. Their faces beamed with love for her. She felt the pressure of a hand on hers.

Saul's hand, warm and pulsating. She smelled his pipe tobacco breath mixed with disinfectant and the fainter undercurrent of urine. She could feel his thoughts. The two of them were dancing to an Anatolian folk melody. A violin and a flute. They whirled and whirled. Her children appeared in a blur, then vanished. Only Hannah's face became momentarily clear. Her mother and father, smiling, held out their arms to her. Time passed. Her breathing grew rough, and she struggled for breath.

Saul had dozed off. When he woke up, his hand was numb from holding hers, but she grasped his with an iron-like grip. She had a peaceful expression, as if she were merely enjoying a restful sleep.

51.

She was pushing as hard as she could. She cried out with pain. A nurse rubbed her belly with a circular motion. "Almost there, honey. Just a little more. Push. Keep on. Yes. That's it. Deep breath. Again. Open your mouth and breathe out. Deep breath. Push."

White ceiling. White walls. A window that looked out onto a brick wall.

Push. Push. Tired. Breathe out. Deep breath in and out. She felt as if she were being torn apart.

"Good girl. You're almost there, honey. Keep on pushing. Almost there."

Hannah reached to feel for the baby's head, but the nurse pulled her hand away.

So tired. Thirsty. The nurse held a glass of water to her lips. Patted her forehead. Massaged her belly. A final push and she felt it slip out and heard it cry. A little later she held the baby against her breast. It was a girl! She had dark hair and Sean's blue eyes. An immense joy flooded Hannah. She had given birth to a new life. At that instant nothing else mattered.

ABOUT THE AUTHOR

MARIA ESPINOSA is the author of five novels, including *Longing*, which won the 1996 American Book Award; two collections of poetry, one of which was praised by Anaïs Nin as being "very sincere and direct and rich in feeling"; and a translation of George Sand's *Lélia*. The 2010 winner of the PEN Oakland/Josephine Miles Literary Award, she has taught creative writing and contemporary literature at New College of California and English as a Second Language at City College of San Francisco. She lives in Albuquerque, New Mexico, and has one daughter. Her website is www.mariaespinosa.com.